Crossing The Dream Line

Also by Michèle Vachon Beaudin

Crossing the 50 Yard Line

ISBN 978-0-615-17157-9

Seven women, seven different stories. Three hundred and fifty years of life between them, but all feeling too young to give up or give in, some faced with life decisions. Stories of running away from a painful past, present or future. Stories of self-discovery by women who got lost somewhere between childhood and now.

Seasons On Lookout Mountain

ISBN 978-0-615-32453-1

With stunning images and beautiful prose, the author unveils the incredible beauty and serenity of Lookout Mountain throughout the seasons.

The Mountain

ISBN 978-0-615-33963-4

The author captures the unique beauty and spirituality of Scaly Mountain, North Carolina, with her original photographs accompanied by the prose the images inspired.

Crossing The Dream Line

Michèle Vachon Beaudin

immiges & words press
Tallahassee, Florida, USA

© 2010 by immiges & words press
All rights reserved.

Book design by Michèle Vachon Beaudin

www.immigesandwords.com
www.immiges.com

michele@immiges.com

ISBN 978-0-9826877-0-3

Library of Congress Control Number: 2010934674

Printed in the United States of America

First Edition

Author's Foreword

This story starts ten years after seven different women faced their life's half century landmark in my previous novel, "Crossing the 50 Yard Line". These same women are now confronting a new, even more significant decade.

Just when they thought 50 was a difficult line to cross, they encounter 60, an age when not everything is possible anymore. As the women celebrate their birthday, they realize that society now brands them as senior citizens, assumed to have major health problems and deciding that they no longer qualify for much else besides social security. However, in spite of the sounds of doors slamming shut all around them, they know there is still more life out there and they want their share of it.

While the last novel explored their individual thoughts and how they tried to circumvent their feelings of loss and fear for the future, this one has the characters meet by one of those coincidences that never cease to amaze us. They each discover that regardless of their social or economic background, most women are faced with similar challenges and share the same hopes and dreams. This chapter of their lives is more about exploring the possibilities of this new decade, and less about mourning losses of self and youth as were their previous stories.

Over the ten years since their last important birthday, some have found comfort and serenity in new places and lifestyles but wonder how long it can last. Others have finally resolved that no one will ever really need them again and find themselves yearning for something new, something that is missing in each of their lives, maybe an attempt to rekindle if only a touch of the excitement and challenges that used to fill their younger days.

Some sadly recognize that while women fought to be respected and treated equally for decades, the road is still paved with obstacles and the same prejudices often raise their heads. Their most important realization, however, is that life can take you to new places, let you explore new paths once your mind opens up to all its possibilities.

You may find some opinions or views the characters hold or talk about, may at times appear inconsistent, even contradictory. My aim was not for this to be a channel for my own beliefs, although some appear between the lines. The goal was to try and expose as many facets of each woman as I could for the reader to see.

While I got my inspiration from the countless women I have met over the last six decades, the characters in this story are solely born from my imagination and are not based on any persons in the realms of reality.

I dedicate this book to new friends, Barbara, Cathy, Mike just to name a few, who were there on my adoptive Lookout Mountain to carry me across that dream line and to all women who, like me won't give up and still wonder what opportunity waits around the corner.

Special thanks to my husband and partner Gene Stuckey. His help and support were a huge factor in getting this book published and to my extraordinary children and grand children whose accomplishments make us very proud and who remain close in spite of distances.

Contents

JULIE

Saturday morning. Finally, I'm going to have fun. It's been a while. I was up early and didn't sit at the table with my coffee until now and it's almost 11 o'clock. I think everything is under control and, from what I heard, everyone is looking forward to the party. Well, here I am with nothing left to do but hope everyone comes up with whatever they said they'd come up with and the guests show up. I have my new 'Theresa design' dress ready to wear and have asked the bartender to spike my coffee. Life is good.

I finally had a chance to talk to some of the guests. A very interesting group of people and all women, well... except for the Mr. in the Mr. and Mrs. I find it interesting how women seem to travel by themselves more than men do. I guess men are probably like my own mate who won't go anywhere unless I drag him, so he certainly wouldn't vacation by himself, unless it involved 24 hour golf and still, he'd probably drag a few of his regular golfing buddies along for the ride.

I'm not sure Betsy or Patricia will show up. They don't look like the party types. Even Lucy doesn't strike me as the fun sort. But, who knows, vacations are a time when people should do something out of the ordinary. Clara has been mostly hanging around the

1

beach, or sitting near the pool but maybe her friend will encourage her to loosen up and party. Then again, the woman she came to meet here doesn't strike me as a hoot. Oh well, we'll see.

Another woman checked in this morning as I was getting my 'special' coffee. She's nice looking, elegant but not overly so. A bit too haughty looking for my liking, maybe. Her highlighted brown hair is short, but it seems to be a recent change: every so often, she shakes her head as if to chase strands of hair from her face... which there aren't any. Interesting. She had a wedding ring, but no husband in sight. I wonder what's up with her. She kept looking around as though looking for someone. If it's a man, he surely didn't register here.

I don't think we've had an affair at the inn since I've been here. Not unless Mr. and Mrs...?

I had to stop writing I was laughing so hard. Not possible. Definitely no affair there. OK, I'm being a bit catty and judgmental, but really, they are really not the types! Anyway, affairs are better consummated in anonymous hotel chains where one is less likely to be spotted or meet someone they know. Oh well, I'll just have to settle for interesting, albeit not exciting guests.

2 PM. Christopher stopped by to see if I needed any help. I know better. I think he's pissed that I didn't

invite him and Theresa to my party, at least not yet. I thought about it, but quite frankly, this is supposed to be more of a business affair for neighborhood businesses and guests. The truth? I tend to feel intimidated when family is around at times like that: one, I can't talk (or exaggerate) about them if they are there and two, there are topics of conversation I can discuss with strangers that should not reach the ears of family members. So, he'll just have to deal. Besides, I haven't NOT invited them so maybe I'll change my mind.

Anyway, I told him I'd stop by later to see the kids and talk to Theresa. Sometimes I wish I would have given birth to such a sweet daughter... but I know the family gene pool just doesn't match that profile. No one is really sweet where I come from. Just busy, polite and usually wealthy. Well, except maybe sis Carrie. Nah, even she got over the hippy'ish, earthy attitude and now runs her own trendy whole food store. I'm sure Theresa will understand and even if she doesn't, she'll be ok with it. I find it great that such a strong minded woman can be so sweet, but I know for a fact that she doesn't put up with any shit from my darling son. That said, I feel a bit guilty since she helped find the music and made me this awesome dress... so, really, maybe I will change my mind, what the hell...

CROSSING THE DREAM LINE

I better get myself in gear if I want to see the babies and still be ready for cocktails at five.

##

Part 1

The Years Between

JACKIE

I'm sorry. Yes, I'm sorry. I know I've said it a million times before, but I'm sorry. I'm sorry I could never do anything right, or make any good decisions. I'm sorry I messed up so many people's lives. I'm sorry.

Kathy, Stephanie, I love you so much I never knew how my moving away hurt you so. I'm sorry. Peter. I feel I did nothing but use you over the years. I wanted more than you could give, but was unable to find out what it was I wished for. I'm just so sorry.

And Tommy, you, who took the time to rescue me when I was down. Who took me back to my life and still cared. I'm sorry. I never meant to get pregnant when we were kids. I loved you so much, but I really didn't mean to. Marrying you may have completely destroyed your life. Then I swear I didn't choose to be lured by the excitement of the city and leave you, but I thought I could make a better life for myself and the kids. I'm oh so sorry.

I was so selfish. I never realized that what I was doing was all for myself. I really believed that it would be for the good of everyone. I really did.

Sorry kids for the time in Bermuda. I know you were miserable and missed your dad and friends, but I was so scared about what could happen to you in Manhattan once you were teenagers. I knew I could barely control my own life and genuinely thought the more peaceful island life would be good for you.

And Peter. How can you ever forgive me for taking advantage of your good nature? I love you in more ways than one, but was never really in love with you. I had given up on myself and needed a safe haven. You provided everything I needed for me to survive, but you didn't know how to love and I cried many nights, the woman in me wanting to be in love again. I was so lonely for most of the years we were together; I stayed because I thought the kids could not handle yet another break in the family. You are still standing by me no matter what. I know it's unfair and I'm sorry.

I'm so sorry. How could I ever think that what I was doing was for the kids and a better life? I don't know. They barely talk to me now.

I'm sorry about what happened in Paris and London and wherever else I tried to find some solace. I never told you what I survived there because I never trusted you to understand: I was expected to be the strong person to keep it all together, but I really never could. I looked arrogant and was even cruel at times, but, if it makes everyone feels better, I was never able to be happy myself.

That's why I can now say goodbye and know that you will understand that I can't be sorry anymore. I need to be at peace with myself and the world around me, and since you are all so successful in your own lives, maybe I can smile and think that I may, in some small way, have something to do with it.

I love you all oh so much and can never express how sorry I am for my failures and the havoc they wreaked in your lives.

I know that after a few weeks, you will all be fine and go on with your lives as if I'd never been a part of it.

Just know I always wanted the best for you and love you forever and go on to a new realm, knowing that you cared and that you will soon be able to smile again.

Love forever,
Mom, Jackie…

##

"I can do this." Jackie paused, 'I can do this. I know I can do this." She was sitting at her vanity, looking in the mirror, trying to project an image of domestic bliss. It wasn't working.

She wanted to scream. When would all of this ever end? Why was she still around? Why, on earth was she still here? There was a party going on downstairs and she was required to attend, look good and smile. Not so hard, one would think, but Jackie didn't think she could do it.

Almost ten years after the disastrous turn of events of her half century adventure, she was finally waking to a semblance of her old self. It was becoming easier to pretend that life was great but she didn't have it quite down pat yet.

The road up, from where she was found in Brighton so many years ago, had been harsh and steep. As was usual with her family, everyone pretended nothing had happened and that all was normal. Maybe it was, but not in her head. She had played along, cooking, shopping, sleeping, even organizing some extravagant, not to mention expensive weddings for the girls, but her heart hadn't been in it.

Peter, her husband, whose very nature was sedate and calm had just assumed that the experience she had overseas, together with the passing of time, had brought a new maturity to his wife. He was certain that all fires were extinguished and that they would walk, side by side, into the shadow of death holding hands, happy forever.

She had never told. He knew nothing. Nothing of her Paris lover, nothing of her brush with violence and drugs, nothing of the desperation she had felt at the time. Even Tommy, the ex-husband who had come to pick her up from the depth of despair she had fallen into on the beach of Brighton, never questioned or demanded to know the reasons for the breakdown. She had never called Janice again, her best friend from the years spent in New York, the one person she had turned to for help on that fateful night.

As usual she had chosen the loneliest path to deal with the consequences of her fall. Her daughters were now married and had successful careers and children to keep them occupied. Kathy had made a beeline for New York as soon as she graduated and was now settled in a New Jersey suburb, working in Manhattan for an advertising agency. Stephanie was closer but too busy with her veterinarian practice to visit. She rarely saw either of them and had to stretch her mind to develop any interest in the three grandsons they had produced.

Her own nearly estranged sister had increased the space between them by over a thousand miles, moving to Arizona soon after their parents died. Jackie never contested the will that left her dad's Scottsdale house and most everything else to her sister. Her older sibling was, after all, the one who had faithfully followed in their parents' footsteps so it was right for them to recompense her accordingly. As for local friends, after returning from her overseas' ordeal, Jackie had not reconnected with them and they faded away both in her mind and from her address book. She simply went along with whatever Peter decided was good for her and was civil to the friends, mostly acquaintances he occasionally brought home.

Looking back at her nearly sixty years of existence, Jackie now recognized that all she had done was to create a family dynamic to resemble that of the family she had grown up in. Her passive aggressive mother, her silent father, the lack of empathy from any members of the family towards one another, all was replicated perfectly here. She thought she had broken the mold, but in retrospect, she had carried the dysfunction endured as a child to a higher level. She grew up alone and was still alone in spite of all the live bodies surrounding her.

She no longer had the basement where she so excitedly had cycled, worked out and lifted weights to get fit and as attractive as she could for her 50th birthday trek. Peter had found it wise to build a new house for her, farther from the city, but with all the amenities anyone could have dreamed of, short of a gym. The basement served as a home theatre and game room. No more exercise videos or equipment. She didn't need them anymore. Jackie had lost her craving for food along with that for life, so weight was no longer a problem. Peter had also bought her an expensive foreign sports car which she really never cared for, but had to use since every errand required miles of driving. His generosity reminded her of the new bedroom suite, the fur coat and new clothes her own mother would buy for her whenever she voiced sadness or depression. The idea was that, if you bought material things for people, they would love you and, by instilling guilt and gratitude, you would also be spared from dealing with any potentially upsetting feelings and emotions.

Jackie opened the secret drawer under her vanity and read the letter of apology which she had written to her family only a year after coming back from what was to be her half century birthday present. No. They were never going to read it and she wondered why she had kept it. Probably to remind herself of all the resentment she had seeded around her and a lesson on how to avoid making the same mistakes again. She feared, however, that someone would find it and not understand her state of mind at the time. Not that she didn't mean what she wrote or didn't still have those feelings, but because it would show a side of her she chose to keep hidden from her family. It was enough that Janice had heard her desperation and that Tommy had found her lost in Brighton, so close to fading away, she didn't want anyone else to know.

Tommy, her high school sweetheart and ex-husband had been the one to come to her when she had reached bottom. He had cleaned her up and sent her home to pretend to be over what everyone referred to as 'just a phase'. Tommy had tried to stay in contact, but apart from their crossing paths at the girls' weddings, she shut the door to any kind of friendship.

Now, here she was, all dolled up and facing one of Peter's ideas of entertainment.

##

Coming down the stairs, she spied on her reflection in an enormous, cathedral-size window over the front door. She saw that her hair, skillfully twisted at the nape, and the somber black silk dress gave her an adequate, elegant public image. She took a deep breath to compose herself before facing the guests. Most were Peter's work colleagues and their wives. Some were neighbors she occasionally said hello to, but overall there was no one at the party she cared to get to know better or even talk to.

She painted a smile on her face, walked through the small clusters of conversations and made her way to the kitchen. Olga, the housekeeper, compliments of Peter, was helping the caterer sort out the dishes and walked in and out of the living room with hors-d'oeuvres and drink trays. Jackie knew her own presence was not required, but she felt more comfortable here than in the living room where everyone was discussing the weather, their various vacation destinations, their children or golf.

Over the last few years, her tolerance for small talk had lessened to the point where she sometimes appeared rude to people who approached her just to chat. She didn't care about subjects that didn't teach her anything new or challenge her mind. Avoiding conversations was now her best defense against annoyance and boredom.

She grabbed a couple of canapés and thought of reaching for one of the glasses now filled with wine but held back. Ever since her encounter with binge drinking while in Europe, she had stayed away from alcohol as much as she could. She knew the letter in the drawer was written after an empty bottle of wine had joined another in the recycling bin and couldn't imagine what she may have done had she not passed out, face down on her desk. She did not want to reach that desperate place drinking often opened the door to.

Finding nothing for her to do in the kitchen, Jackie rejoined the guests, some of whom were now discussing an issue encountered with some office computer snafu. She tried to look interested, but bowed out as soon as the occasion presented itself.

14

Olga was calling her discretely asking about the whereabouts of a particular platter.

Sometimes she thought Olga, the middle aged Russian woman, knew more about her than her own family. She seemed to sense when a mood string had to be broken and gently provided the distraction to change the path her mind was bent on taking. Jackie answered the woman's question and took advantage of this diversion to sneak out the back door for some fresh air.

Fall had definitely completed its cycle, leaving the air crisp and cool with a hint of winter yet to come. The scent of leaves blanketing the lawn was intoxicating. Jackie shivered and smiled. Rust, gold and red, the crispy carpet of colors brought peace in her heart. She walked around the flower garden and the pool, both now prepared for the first frost, and reached her favorite spot. After the move, she had purchased a carved wooden bench and proceeded to place it facing away from the house, overlooking the forest where the property ended. That was where she sat now, feeling the cold of the wooden slats beneath her thin dress, smiling again, recalling the argument she had with the landscaper who thought a bench facing away from his artwork would destroy any harmonious mood he was trying to create. She had stuck to her guns and was glad she did. This, after all, was her only personal contribution to the new house.

Jackie was sure no one was missing her at the party, so she just tried to free her mind and enjoy the temporary respite from the crowd. In the darkness of the forest, she saw something move out of the corner of her eye. A deer, she thought, secretly yearning to follow its trail and maybe find a purpose along the way.

##

The first thing Jackie had done when the numbness of the past started to dissipate, was to go out and find avenues where she could forget about her life while learning something new and somehow keep on breathing day after day. Going back to school as her daughter Kathy had suggested was out of the question. Her school days were filled with bad memories of tedious work and boredom. She also had no interest in sitting in a lecture hall listening to someone, usually a man, who, in her opinion, was there solely to hear the sound of his own voice.

Finding a job was not an option. Peter now earned so much that she would have to pay her entire income in taxes, considering the fact that she was now practically unemployable and would fare little more than minimum wage. After all these years in the fast lane, she had to face a tragic reality: she could never go back to being a successful, respected and well paid woman in a business world that had no room for older women. Besides, things had changed. What had been an exciting career 30 years ago, meeting new people, power lunches and entertaining out of town clients had turned into men and women sitting in front of computers for hours on end with no link to any sort life forms apart from the ones technology offered.

Jackie had started haunting museums and galleries. She and Peter attended an assortment of openings, galas and fund raisers. Her husband had liked this new Jackie, but she knew all those were just distractions. She was still bored. She had no talent of her own, artistically speaking, and no longer found any motivation to get into any sports or exercise regimen. She didn't even participate in the process of building the new house. An interior designer was hired to complete the project. None of the new home décor reflected her personality: the whole style was ostentatious, the furniture looking like something out of a show room and the art matching the sofas. As far as Jackie was concerned, it had no soul. It was a dead shell, perfect in fact for someone who had been feeling like such for so long. She was grateful for Olga. She knew she could never have maintained this house on her own or at all. She felt this building was a hotel, a temporary place to sleep until something better came along; at least she hoped something would.

When the art world faded from her interest, Jackie took on the battle of the bookstores. Going back to her favorite haunt in Milwaukee was nearly an hour drive, but the new ones in her artificial neighborhood were too sterile. She had tried them all. She sometimes even drove up to Madison to walk on State Street and soak herself into some sort of intellectual bath without the pain of research or homework. This is where she met Lucy who, in spite of looking a bit frumpy and somewhat furtive, had immediately drawn Jackie's attention. The chance meeting happened in a small, quaint book store where Lucy was reading an account of some African mission she had participated in.

With nothing better to do, Jackie sat through the reading and, feeling guilty for not knowing anything about the novel or its author, purchased the book and waited to have it autographed. While standing in the short line, she read the woman's biography and found her adventure, clocked after her 50th birthday, had taken place the same year as her own escapade to Paris. They were the same age, they had both run away from home. She looked up from the book and judged that she would never have guessed her age since Lucy definitely had a more traditional older woman look. The coincidence, however, triggered some interest. Since there were only two other customers behind her, she let them go ahead and waited until she could take time to talk with the women.

It was surprising how such a plain looking woman could be so interesting. Having nothing better to do, Jackie invited Lucy to join her for coffee as soon as the other woman had completed her duty to the publisher. Lucy gladly accepted. They walked a few doors down and spent what turned out to be nearly two hours exchanging basic information and discussing Lucy's book. They did not have much in common, except age and perhaps that they both had two daughters. However, Jackie was desperate for companionship that wasn't home grown, and finding out that Lucy lived by herself with no one to go home to could mean someone to potentially share some time with.

They exchanged phone numbers and went their separate ways, neither woman never really expecting to meet again.

A few weeks later Jackie was once again in her favorite Milwaukee book store on 76th street, when she saw Lucy, reading from her book which was called, unoriginally, "My year in Africa". Jackie thought she would have had a title like "Jumpstarting the Next 50 in Africa" or something a little snazzier, but she had read the book and while she found it as unoriginal as its title, she enjoyed the details of an existence in a place that couldn't be any more different than American life as she knew it. She also related to the tide the other woman had to ride before coming home to a reality she could finally deal with.

As she was leaving, Lucy spotted Jackie in the coffee shop and waved. She walked over to her table and a new conversation began. An hour later, the women made plans, this time firm ones for lunch the following week. Both women were becoming more comfortable with each other and the conversation had turned to more personal subjects. Lucy wanted to know more about Jackie's Paris experience, but the story had never been told and Jackie was not ready to share. Anyone watching those women would have thought how unlikely these two could ever be friends. But they hadn't reached that stage yet.

The date chosen for their future meeting coincided with Lucy's 60th birthday. The self-effacing woman said this was no big deal. Her family was celebrating on the previous weekend so the day chosen for their lunch date was just going to be an ordinary one for her.

When they left the restaurant, Jackie noticed Lucy's car and was embarrassed to get into her over priced convertible. She asked her new friend where she lived and suggested she could pick her up since her apartment was on the way and they could help the environment by carpooling. Lucy quickly agreed, always fearing that the next trip in her ancient compact would be the last.

##

LUCY

"Rock-a-by Lucy" Lucy smiles at the thought as she swings the chair back and forth on her daughter's porch where she can gaze at Lake Muskego and day dream. "Where have those ten years gone", she wonders, remembering her last turn of the decade and how she ran away from it all. Today is her 60th birthday party and the family gathering is quite tame except for the kids running around the grounds playing who knows what game. She sighs appreciating the quiet moment when the children make no any urgent demands on her. She knows it won't last.

"Grandma, Grandma" Danielle calls out. Lucy smiles. Her granddaughter is now nearly as tall as she is, almost a teenager, but still as sweet as she was the day she had said goodbye to her at the airport ten years ago. That phase of her life flashes before her eyes: the realization that, at fifty, she had become someone people talked about in the past tense or in reference to her relationship to someone else. She thinks of her mission in North Africa, the desert, Fatiha, the fears and torments she had subjected herself to during that year. She nods quietly to herself, remembering that, all in all, she came home a person in her own right, no longer an old, comfortable shoe to be used by the family as needed.

Lucy gives her granddaughter the hug she came for and Danielle smiles, knowing that they share a bond stronger than one of a granddaughter - grandmother; they are attached at the soul.

"Are you coming with us for a boat ride?" the child asks with starry eyes. "My friend Jacob from school is coming. He's cool!" Lucy takes her hand. "I really would like to meet him, but you know me and boats... huh... not so good. Go along. You can come and introduce him later." Danielle takes her hand back and turns to run to the dock. "OK, see you later. Can't wait for you to see what we got you!"

Lucy resumes her rocking and thinks about all the years that passed, wondering if she should have any regrets. She decides that no. She did what she had to do and no one could have predicted what happened later.

##

After a year abroad, Lucy returned to Milwaukee which, she observed while her husband was driving back from the airport, had changed very little. At first, fear gripped her heart: things would be the same and that year would be lost, a wasted year in a life already more than half way to its end. The first thing she saw as she walked into her home was the old piano. She no longer associated with it: the instrument was still there but its symbol of her middle aged self had faded. It was also in a far worse state than it was when she had left it, whereas she had been restored to life. In fact, she noted, the entire house was covered with dust as if abandoned by its owners. Was that what her fate was to be? To keep toiling in this old house and be at everyone's beck and call… again. She shivered.

Lucy had hoped Rob would have looked forward to her return, ready as she was, to start a new life together, but the house spoke of a different man. She looked at him, the husband who, according to her daughter Rebecca, had been drinking the year away. Something gripped at her heart. This was not the charming fiancé she had married so many years ago. At only 55, he had the face of a sad old man who had given up on himself. She struggled with feelings of guilt.

Karen, Rebecca and the kids had arrived as Rob and Lucy were staring at one another, trying to find the words that would start a conversation. After a sober family dinner of take-out Chinese food and many comforting hugs from the grandchildren, Lucy was sad to see the girls leave her alone to face a husband she no longer recognized.

Disheartened, she went in the kitchen and started washing the dishes, which, she saw, included glasses and plates evidently in the sink for days, leftovers glued to the bottom. Once this was done, she walked into the living room where Rob was sitting on the couch and studied the family pictures hanging over the dusty fireplace mantel. It was a shock to see that Rob looked exactly the way he had for some years. For the first time, she realized that he may have been in the same painful place she was in the year before. However, because communication between them had expired so many years ago, she had never suspected. Neither ever talked to the other about their doubts, fears or feelings, about their lives or the state of their marriage.

A wave of affection mixed with pity brought her to join her husband on the couch. She reached for his hand but Rob got up to refill his drink and sat back in the recliner where he found the remote and turned the television on. She sighed, got up and went to bed, barely recognizing the bedroom she had left the year before. She quickly fell asleep, jet lagged and mentally exhausted while her husband spent the night in the living room. The television was still on when Lucy came downstairs the next day but Rob was gone.

A few weeks passed with her busily attempting to bring the house into some sort of order. Then one day, while doing the laundry, a ticket fell out of Rob's pants pocket. She sighed. It appeared that gambling was also how her husband had been spending his free time and money. Lucy suspected something like that since he had been reluctant to give her a credit card or even enough money to cover everyday expenses. She had, however, never involved herself in their financial affairs, so she assumed he needed time to get back to their former routine. The next day, while cleaning his desk in the den, she was going to close a drawer left ajar when she saw unopened envelopes, many looking suspiciously like bills. Her heart pounded in her chest as she opened them and found bank statements with red balances, payment reminders and threatening letters from creditors asking for money. She then frantically searched the files and read through other papers scattered on top of the desk. She collapsed on a chair as she read the contract for a second mortgage on the house.

She was devastated. She had implicitly trusted Rob, naively giving him power of attorney for the year she would be away, never imagining that this would be the end result. That mistake had her facing an empty bank account as well as credit cards all over their limits. When her husband got home, she sought an explanation but he had none. He became angry and told her that if she didn't like his ways, she could just go back to wherever she had been for the last year. He left the house, slamming the door behind him. Lucy finally understood that she had come home to a stranger, one who felt saddled with a woman, there only to nag and criticize. She also saw that her marriage had been over long before she had left for Africa. Now was time to face the truth. She went to the bedroom and packed her bags, once and for all, done with this house and her old life. Lucy was surprised at the sense of relief she felt when she left the house which would never be her home again.

Without a car or money, she called her daughter Karen who invited her to stay at her apartment downtown. Karen, the daughter who never seemed to settle down, had done just so while Lucy was gone. This refuge served as a transition between the illusion of security in her marriage, the fear of becoming dependant or homeless and the joy of reinventing her life. Mother and daughter were amazed at how close they would become, after years of disagreeing on most subjects. Rebecca, her oldest, had always been her rock, solid, predictable, never needing special attention, someone her mother had come to view as a good friend. However, Lucy was shocked when she started receiving disapproving and accusing letters from her while in exile. She had thought the weeks of sitting for the kids while the couple was getting adjusted to parenthood, the help provided whenever it was needed, the years spent worrying and making sure Rebecca finished college, would all count for something. One fateful note had shattered the image she had of her oldest daughter and, in some way, made her self-finding journey and return home more difficult. Their relationship had been strained since Lucy was back, but as the different woman she believed she had become, she was determined to rebuild their bond at any cost.

With a roof over her head, but little else, Lucy tried to find work, pounding the pavement, applying for anything from retail clerk to food service worker. This proved to be an exercise in humility and futility for this woman over fifty with little or no real work experience. She even tried to get her old part time job back as a tour guide for the museum, but interns now filled the post and she needed an income. She learned to use Karen's computer and started transcribing her diary for practice and lack of a better occupation. She volunteered at the local hospital and the food bank hoping that by meeting more people, she would stumble upon an actual paying job.

Rob eventually lost the house and never returned her or the kids' concerned calls. She never demanded nor received support from him. He could barely take care of himself. The divorce was final two years later just as she was starting to earn a living as a medical transcriber.

In the meantime, Karen had met a man and was busy falling in love. Lucy was in the way so she moved into her own place in the suburbs, closer to Rebecca. She bought a small used compact car and started a life that took place between work and family. Working at home was perfect, but since she had given up volunteer activities for work, her social life outside the family was non-existent.

Lucy was by no means back to the hopelessness she had felt about her fiftieth birthday, but she knew something was missing. She spent a lot of time helping Rebecca entertain in her new house on the lake or babysitting Jon Jr. and Danielle. Her daughter's new found prosperity made her proud, but she sometimes felt that her daughter's success made her own failures even more painful. She was losing her determination, the one she had decided upon in Africa that her life should be lived on her terms. But what terms were they? She no longer knew.

Finally in her own place, she went through the boxes of books Rob had sent after he was compelled by creditors to leave the house. Most were the kids' old college textbooks and some romance novels she used to occasionally enjoy. She was about to give up, wrap the whole pile and bring it to the library or thrift shop. Then she came across the one travel adventure story that had set her off on her half century journey.

Lucy abandoned the boxes in the middle of the living room and started reading. She was amazed at how the elated feeling that had made her want to escape at the time could not be recaptured. At her book reading event, the author, spoke about a mission she had been a part of in South America. The woman had been so filled with love and enthusiasm that Lucy was inspired to dream about an escape of her own.

Now, she just stared at the book, wondering how this all came to be. On a whim, she looked up the author on the Internet and found she lived in a town nearby. She emailed the publisher and asked that the woman get in touch with her if possible.

Strangely enough the author remembered Lucy: A shabbily dressed older woman who seemed so needy, she had clung to her well past the end of her book signing event. She wondered what she could possibly want from her now and her curiosity caused her to try and find out.

Lucy's phone rang as she was coming out of the shower. Without her reading glasses, the caller ID was a total blur so she never knew who was calling.

Elaine was the woman's name. Her third adventure book had been published only three months before and she was on a short respite from a whirlwind of book signing tours. The author was intrigued and made room in her life to meet with Lucy, first by curiosity, then, after hearing of Lucy's African experience, as someone who knew the world of books and publishing. Lucy's diary, the stories plus the anecdotes added on to enliven her tale of escape, charmed the now bestselling author who took the frumpy woman from Milwaukee under her wing. Over the following months, between her own engagements, Elaine became a mentor, editor and coach, encouraging Lucy to write a book.

The fear of her family's reaction, faced with some truths they may not want the world to know, had Lucy re-invent her experience to mask the most obvious references to Rob or the kids. Her book was published as she neared her 55th birthday. Lucy, timid at first, eventually became confident enough to do public presentations and start helping other missions recruit volunteers.

Still in the antique rocking chair, Lucy watches the children, parked in the middle of the lake on the family's pontoon boat. She smiles. Even Karen has a family now: a gentle blond baby boy who timidly hangs on to his mom everywhere she goes. Lucy had briefly met his father on one or two occasions. He was Karen's love of her life, but had left the state before Anthony was born, not even attempting to keep in touch with her or his son. "Anthony is Karen's rebound." That's what everyone says, watching the two of them so close and feeding on each other's emotions.

Lucy now recognizes that the changes she made in what was to become a moderately successful book, though not a best seller, had proven unnecessary. She's not sure the kids had noticed their part in it or that they had even read the book. She reflects that her life today is pretty much the same as it was when she was first published. No better, no worse. She doesn't plan on writing another manuscript, but sometimes wonders how long she can live on that one. She will definitely consider early social security when she turns 62 and prays that she remains healthy until then since her health insurance had expired at the same time as her marriage.

For now, Lucy is glad that she was able to quit her data entry job and concentrate on promoting her book. She thinks about Jackie, the unusual woman she met a couple of times at the bookstores. "Why would someone like her want to be friends with someone like me" she wonders. She shrugs it off and leans against the carved wooden headrest of the chair waiting for life to continue.

A glowing sunset is floating on the water, reminding Lucy of her evenings on the roof watching the sun seemingly melting behind the mountains, those tall giants towering over the desert where she lived in their shadow. Darkness soon starts creeping in and the boat crawls back to the dock. The flock of children attacks Lucy and forces her inside the huge dining room where a feast as well as an immense cake is waiting among colorful birthday decorations.

After eating too much, and perhaps drinking a bit more wine than she is accustomed to, she hears the children break into the 'happy birthday' song. Lucy is then assaulted by hugs and kisses, blinding camera flashes popping up from every corner of the room. Then everyone is quiet, waiting for her to receive her 60th birthday present. Solemnly, Rebecca walks over and hands her a thick envelope painted by the children in bright water colors and wrapped in a huge red ribbon.

Lucy is puzzled as she carefully opens the envelope so as to keep the art work intact. She pulls out a stack of paper, reads the cover letter and smiles: One month in a tropical paradise. "We want you to have something to write another book about." Karen laughs. "Yes, and this time, we don't want to be in it." Rebecca chimes in.

Lucy, still off balance, tries to come up with reasons why she can't accept the extraordinary gift. "But I can't get away for a whole month." "Oh mom, you left us for a whole year, what's a month?" Rebecca replies.

Lucy looks at her daughter, expecting some sarcasm or hidden criticism but sees none. Tears tickle her eyes as she suddenly is aware that her children do love her and wish her well. She rises from her chair and embraces them, trying not to cry so as to not upset the grandchildren.

"Thank you. I love you so much," she giggles "and not just because of the gift." She goes around the table, and her feeling is one of peace and contentment. She almost wishes her life could stop now as it would be the culmination of an existence which, in spite of its pain and hardship would end on such a high note.

##

JACKIE & LUCY

The day Jackie and Lucy were to meet for lunch, Jackie picked up her new friend and drove to one of the best restaurants in the city: a fancy bistro, with a panoramic view of the lake, soft music and servers wearing black suit pants, crisp white shirts and bow ties. She wondered if her friend had ever been there.

Lucy had never been in a place like this and was mesmerized by first, the elegance of the restaurant and second, the prices on the menu. She blushed and felt her insides twirl as her spirits dampened. She became acutely aware of her inadequate outfit and calculated that she would have to starve for a week to pay for a meal in this establishment. "I'm not very hungry. I think I'll just have a small salad." She said, hoping to sound sincere.

Jackie laughed. "No way. I'm ordering you to eat one of each item on the menu. In fact, I'll order for you. This is my treat. Happy birthday!"

Lucy smiled shyly. "I can't accept. I've only known you a short time and," she said in a lower tone, "it's too expensive. I really can't accept." "Hey, I can afford it and won't take no for an answer. I have no one to treat to anything these days so you can make me happy by accepting and enjoying the meal." Jackie was smiling but Lucy could tell it was a plea. She was now starting to pierce through the perky façade of this woman and see a very different picture.

Lucy wavered "OK. Thanks. But next time, you come over to my house and I'll make lunch. It won't be like this, but I want to celebrate your birthday too."

Jackie smiled. "Deal".

The server was discretely hovering around the table, filling glasses of water and telling them about the chef's special and the wine selection proposed for each dish. Jackie listened to the young man while observing her companion for reaction to any one particular suggestion. She then ordered light appetizers followed by main courses fit for a king. Lucy was impressed, but tried not to look too unsophisticated.

"So," Jackie asked, "did you have a great birthday party this weekend?" A soft look passed through Lucy's eyes. She smiled. "It was wonderful. Lots of food. Everyone was there. I'm so lucky to have such great kids." She hadn't told Jackie about their father yet. She wasn't ready. "And you know what they got me as a present?" Jackie shook her head, encouraging Lucy to continue. "They gave me a month's vacation in some really fancy island somewhere south, maybe off South America. I'm not sure, but I know it's summer all year long and I'll be there for a whole month." Her excitement was contagious so Jackie encouraged her to elaborate.

"The hotel is called "My Last Dream", Lucy continued. From what I saw on the Internet, it's small but elegant and has very few rooms. The kids thought I would like it because it's not a very commercial resort where everyone is showing off their money and," she laughed, "their girlish figures on the beach. When I saw the picture, I kind of thought of the English Inns with fancy women with umbrellas on the beach you can see in old paintings. But can you believe a month? I didn't think I could get away, but it looks like I can." The mention of English Inns brought back visions of Brighton in Jackie's head, although she remembered very little of it. She quickly chased the images away.

Turning back to the conversation, Jackie was glad to see her friend so ebullient and was happy if not a little jealous of her. She wondered what was in store for her own birthday. "When are you going?" she asked. "After the holidays. I have to busy myself promoting my book for the holiday season, so it won't be for a few months. Besides, I prefer coming home to spring rather than winter. To be honest, at first I was a little scared about leaving the kids again for so long, but now I can't wait!"

The conversation continued over a decadent chocolate lava cake and through the afternoon. Jackie drove Lucy home and both women were glad to have found each other. They were still at the surface stage of their friendship, but that was enough for the two women who needed to live outside the familiar and talk to someone who would judge them for whom they were now without the prejudice of past lifetimes.

##

Jackie's own birthday was accompanied by yet another party composed of people she barely knew. Kathy's family had made the trip from the east coast. Stephanie was there as well, family in tow. The boys had grown so much. Kathy's Jeff was now 6 and Jacob 4 and Stephanie's Jordan had turned 2 just a few days before. As a grandmother, Jackie's maternal instinct had never kicked in. She loved the children but thought that until she could have a rational, adult conversation with them, she didn't really know what to do or say that would amuse or interest those adorable munchkins. Her problem was, 'old age' hadn't kicked in yet either and she didn't see herself as 60 years old, let alone a grandmother. In a way she envied Lucy for being so comfortable with herself and her family.

One-on-one discussions with her husband had become a bit more interesting since she had found conversation outside of Peter. Jackie had told him about Lucy, providing him with as superficial a description as she could: she didn't want him to have her new friend involved in their mutual life. She wanted her all to herself, the only person not associated with her pointless existence. Of course she had mentioned the great birthday present Lucy's children had offered her on her 60th birthday, but not much more.

Now with the whole family and acquaintances together in her oversized living room, she saw a huge cake emerge from the kitchen, one lit up with what looked like a hundred candles. Jackie had to suffer through the flash of cameras as well as everyone's congratulatory hugs and kisses. She didn't think congratulations were in order since she had nothing to do with living that long. However, she smiled on demand, striving to appear like the epitome of carefree happiness.

The hallway was tastefully decorated and a table, bearing a white tablecloth, held gaily wrapped boxes of all sizes. After the candles had been extinguished and the cake distributed among the guests, Jackie was propelled out of the living room by the crowd, encouraged to find what treasures were buried in these packages. She skipped quickly through the bad taste gag presents about old age and moved on to other assorted gifts for which she likely had no use. As she was gracefully thanking the persons whose names were on the cards, she felt a hand on her shoulder. She turned and saw Peter, a huge smile on his face, holding up a flat box, one, Jackie thought, that could hold gloves or jewelry. Carefully unwrapping the one layer of silk paper, she found, and tears welled up in her eyes, a packet of brochures and information for an open vacation package to "My Last Dream". Only her name appeared on the papers. He had listened. Maybe he even knew what was ailing her, but this time he had actually listened and understood how she envied her friend and needed to get away herself.

Everyone in the room disappeared for a moment as she was seeing her husband for the first time again. Peter was waiting for a thank you, but she just hugged him and whispered "I love you" in his ear. She hadn't said it in years. She believed she meant it.

The guests eventually went home and she had an amazing talk with her two daughters, catching up on what seemed like years of just pretending to be listening. It felt like an awakening after a long dreamless sleep. She went to bed with a smile and knew she would call Lucy the next day and invite herself to her house for the promised birthday lunch so they could start planning.

##

BARBARA

Brown leaves were chasing yellow ones, twisting away like mini tornadoes. Whatever trees shed in the winter had done so a while ago but their rejected leaves were still haunting the neighborhood even now when it was time for evergreens to start shedding and replacing their own winter coats. The camellias were budding, many already showing red blooms which had been building momentum since fall.

Barbara was holding a book but her thoughts were as far from this place as they could be. She was back in her old house with the boys, thinking how happy they had been. Now they were scattered all over the country and here she was, finally free but with nothing to do and nowhere to go.

She was relaxing on the screened porch her husband Grant finally agreed to build, after discovering that the North Florida fauna, which includes snakes, alligators and an enormous number of insect species, is a bit aggressive and they would have to spend life indoors lest they build some protective barrier between them and nature. Barbara knew the yellow and green pollen would soon cover every inch of the grounds as well as any table, chair or surface not stored inside. She sneezed as if in anticipation of the allergy season and made a mental note to arrange for an appointment to get her and Grant's allergy shots.

Barbara stretched her arms out and wondered what she would do with her day. After years of catering to everyone else's needs as a social worker, she was finally free to concentrate on her own. Sadly enough, she couldn't think of any, except maybe another cup of tea.

Grant was at work. He had in fact retired a few years ago but decided to look for another job farther south, which, for Barbara, meant farther from the boys. He made less money, but they really didn't need much. They had done well in selling their last property and got a bargain on this one; plus, Grant had invested wisely and their nest egg was secure. This house was close to the city on a small lot surrounded by live oaks which protected them from the sun and nosy neighbors. Grant now walked to work which meant there was no reason to keep her truck and his SUV which he promptly sold as soon as they moved and replaced both with one new compact hybrid. His wife didn't mind: she had hated that truck from the day he had offered it to her and, besides, she didn't go anywhere apart from a weekly trip to the mall or supermarket.

Barbara originally had dreams of travel, visiting the children and, she hoped eventually, grandchildren, but Grant saw no sense in it. He pointed out that now that they lived in the south, there was no need to go anywhere else and the family should consider it a privilege to visit them and escape the cold. And that was that. She was, however keeping some of her retirement money in a special account… just in case.

"Well", she thought, "at least I don't have to drive all those commuting miles anymore." She had originally taken up knitting but it wasn't long before she had run out of people to whom she could gift her timid attempts at creating scarves, hats and vests. Being in Florida didn't help since the season for knitted wear was brief.

This was the year she would turn 60 and Barbara wondered if anyone would do something special for her. Looking back she remembered the events that had surrounded the previous turn of decade, and was therefore not expecting much.

At the time, her mom, who had injured her arm in a fall, had summoned her daughter to come home only a few days after the fateful birthday. It had been a blessing in disguise since Barbara had been growing progressively more annoyed with Grant taking her for granted, his negative attitude and lack of communication. This had given her a legitimate reason to take some time out without rocking the boat.

Her mother was now in a nursing home and no longer recognized her on the few visits back to her home town. Every time the phone rang, she expected to hear that her mom had passed away, trying to gage how she would feel when that happened. Her fear, one she knew was irrational, was that her mom's car mechanic, with whom she had had an upsetting encounter ten years ago, would show up at the funeral. She had never told Grant about John; not that there was anything to tell, but she just didn't think he would understand how she could have been attracted to another man, even though nothing happened. She wanted that secret to follow her to the grave and a face to face with that man may give her away. Gant kept insisting they transfer her mother to a facility closer to home and, with her past in mind, Barbara was seriously considering this alternative.

Grant's parents had both died, his father, about five years ago of a heart attack, his mother, of a broken heart some months later. Barbara always wondered if Donna died because they had been so dependent on each other that she couldn't live without having him around to feed, dress and humor. Can one die of being useless? She shivered at the thought. She had often been told that Grant had married his mother. She didn't see the similarities, but apparently others did.

Her oldest son, Kevin was now well established in Albany, but flying to upper New York State was not easy. There were no direct flights to anywhere from their new hometown, so the visits were rare and always rushed. Her son's first job had worked out, but he had now moved on to work with the state government and was, by all account, doing well. She had heard that politics may be part of his long term goals.

Kevin's wife of four years, Annie, was from Québec. He had met her on a trip to Montréal on his first winter living up north. At first they had seen each other once a month, then every weekend, and finally decided that the cost of commuting was too high and decided to get married. She was a petite woman with short brown hair but long bangs hiding half her dark eyes. Her skin was translucent and she had the look of a Madonna. Annie's smile lit up a room and Barbara had fallen in love with her future daughter-in-law as soon as she had met her on one of the rare visits to see her son. Her spunk and spontaneity were contagious and she sang her English in a lilt that charmed this woman who was glad her son had left his comfort zone and ventured where life and love lived in a brighter light, something she, herself, could never do.

Grant was not thrilled about Kevin marrying a foreigner and was also quite grumpy about flying out of the country for the wedding. However, he reasoned that this was family no matter what and there was duty attached to that bond. Barbara secretly thought that once he got a passport, he may get a taste for out of country travel. That part didn't pan out, but the wedding was all Barbara had dreamed of for her son. While Annie's family spoke little English, she herself was quite fluent. Her parents certainly knew how to entertain. The flower garden of their city home, with a view of the Mont Royal, afforded the perfect venue for the reception. Grant only realized his son would marry in a Catholic church as the limo, rented for the occasion, drove him to this extraordinarily ornate cathedral downtown. He came close to backing out, but relented. He was a proud man who had never liked looking foolish. He drew the line, however, at kneeling during the ceremony. Later, while Barbara was meeting what was now a new extension to the family, Grant sat on a garden chair keeping an eye on her and occasionally glancing at his Blackberry.

The young couple now lived in a suburb of Albany and had a small cottage in the Laurentians for winter and summer sports. Barbara thought it was odd since there are many vacation resorts closer to Albany, but her son explained that Annie had spent most of her summers in those mountains as a child and still had many friends in the area. They also wanted to keep a foot in each country which, down the line could afford them dual citizenship, allowing them to work in either place. His new bride was a physical therapist so she had no difficulties finding a job in her adopted country and the couple appeared happy. While she never mentioned this to them, Barbara wished they would give her grandchildren, or at least one grandchild but that hadn't happened yet.

Patrick had reluctantly come to the wedding, flying from California where he had remained after graduating from UCLA. He was involved in Real Estate and appeared to be doing well as he offered his brother a honeymoon vacation to Hawaii as a wedding present. It was hard for Barbara to get close to her younger son since his telephone calls were always vague and his short visits during the holidays gave her no clue as to the life he had built for himself there. He was alone. No girlfriend that she knew of. She worried about that. He was an intelligent, handsome young man. Every time they had voiced their interest in visiting, he always found an excuse to keep them away.

##

"Today will be a... nothing... day" Barbara thought, getting back to the present. She smiled at the decision and started reading again. She had given up the sappy romance novels she used to favor for more challenging mysteries. She even read the occasional biography, provided it was about someone she liked and agreed with, politically or socially. No controversial or cutting edge books for this conservative woman.

While the thermometer had plunged to near freezing the previous night, it was now almost 75'. She took her sweater off, lifted her head and remembered to enjoy the light nature noises of early spring before the incredible cacophony of summer critters began.

Grant came in early that day, catching Barbara still enjoying what bit of warmth was left on this late afternoon. She was puzzled but watched him as he walked from the driveway. "Hey, you're early" she said as he came close to where she sat. "Yes," Grant replied, "a power failure at the office." He paused, took his jacket off and moved a chair to sit by his wife. "You know, I thought we could go out to eat at that new Steak house on Apalachee, they have an early bird special and I hear it's quite good."

Barbara looked up at him to see if he had been drinking, but he looked fine. "Sure. If you want to. I guess I better get changed." He nodded as she rose from her chair and walked inside the house to find a more appropriate dinner outfit.

The restaurant was quiet on this weekday afternoon; they were seated immediately. "What's the occasion?" Barbara couldn't help asking while the server hovered around the table waiting for them to decide on an entrée. Grant looked at her as if she were a nuisance ignoring her until he had ordered their meal and the server had left. "Well, I was told today I had to take vacation days if I didn't want to lose them." His wife looked up, surprised. Grant didn't really 'do' vacations. He just took a day once in a while to putter around the house, a week for out of town weddings or funerals, but real vacations, not really.

"Here's the thing. It's your birthday soon and I thought maybe we should celebrate early since I have to take that time before the summer. What do you think?" Barbara wasn't sure what she was supposed to think something about, but she always found that agreeing always worked. "Sure, sounds good." "Ok, so here it is." He pulled out a computer print-out from his jacket pocket and handed it to her.

"What is that?" she asked. "Well, it's a trip to a vacation resort. I know you've been wanting to get away for a while, so I figured maybe we can go to a nice beach, that's it." Barbara was beyond surprised, bordering on shocked: maybe he won the trip or maybe someone gave him a good deal, maybe, and this made her frown, his doctor gave him bad news after his annual checkup. In any case she wasn't going to pass it up. But, she wondered, what was the deal with the expensive restaurant, even on an early bird basis?

"Happy birthday, Barbara." Grant said, loud enough for the server to hear, obviously hoping for a free dessert. "My birthday isn't until September. We've barely passed Christmas. But that's OK." She bent over and kissed him on the cheek. Thank you Grant. I'm glad we'll be able to go somewhere together. What do you know about his place?"

As it happened, he had been told by a colleague that it was a reasonably priced resort where you could go and no one bothered you for tips or lured you into tourist traps at every stop. That particular hotel was one of the least expensive on the island. He had managed to get a deal on the Internet and they were going to "My Last Dream". An odd name for a tropical resort, but the price was right and it sounded good.

Barbara and Grant remained quiet for the rest of the meal. She was more comfortable in this familiar silence but couldn't help wonder what was behind her husband's newfound thoughtfulness. Years of marriage however, had taught her not to ask.

##

BETSY

The baby's eyes are shining as though eager to laugh at the first nonsense the adult will throw at him. Betsy giggles. The boy mimics her grin and drool rolls down his chin.

"Can you say GraaaaaannMaaa," she asks, mouth wide open, to show him how to make the sounds.

He looks more puzzled than interested, arms and legs randomly flaying as though bouncing a large imaginary ball on his belly. Betsy secures the diaper then snaps the soft yellow pajamas back together. She picks up the baby from the changing table and gathers him up in her arms, holding him as close as she can, given how small he is. He was born prematurely, not quite eight months into the pregnancy and, at three months, has only recently grown to where he can be handled and played without fear of breaking him.

His nursery contains every stimulating picture, colorful toy and piece of furniture any baby could ever want. There are other objects, some electronic in nature, most of which are totally foreign to Betsy. She muses that there was probably more money invested in this one room than in the entire house where she lives.

Mary Beth walks in on her mother and smiles. "I don't know how you do it, but Alex seems to be so content when he's with you."

Betsy turns to face her own baby daughter. Mary Beth looks perfect, as usual, but her mom knows how tired and stressed she is. The night feedings, the special care and only two months to recuperate were not enough, plus, she had insisted on breast feeding in spite of the doctors' advice. She had trimmed her hours at the clinic, starting earlier and leaving to be with Alex after his afternoon nap. The nanny search had been fruitless so far, which is why Betsy filled in whenever she could. "I'll take over, mom." I know you have to go back to work yourself and Ben will be back soon anyway.

Betsy looks down at her grandson and a prayer rises in her heart: let him be happy, she asks of God. The baby starts kicking his feet against her and puts his weight forward so his mother will pick him up, and, as all children do, immediately forgets everyone else in the room. She passes the baby on to her daughter and quietly leaves the room.

"Ten years," Betsy thinks. "It's been over ten years since I crashed at Susan's apartment". She had never looked back. Life had taken a turn she never could have predicted or imagined and here she is, close to another landmark decade, wondering how long this life can last. She smiles, remembering her flight to New York, the first she had been on, ever, and gains a new respect for the 50 year old woman she was then, the one who thought her life was over.

Her mind wanders as she walks the two chilly blocks to the subway and memories, some good, some like wounds that won't heal, take over in what is left of her tired mind. She catches a glimpse of herself in the windows as the train races in the station and smiles. Her hair is long, tied in a loose bun; her exposed face is wrinkled, but fresh and serene. "I'm a long way from this curly haired country bumpkin matron who showed up on her daughter's doorstep." Her gray tweed woolen coat is simple, splashes of color provided only by the bright scarf one of the new girls knitted for her at la Casa. She is comfortable in her body, thinner now that New York has taught her to walk. She tries to remember when she last drove a car and can't.

Working with Father Pascal at La Casa de Maria has literally been a godsend. Raising her children had been rewarding but mostly stressful, always worrying about everyone's happiness and safety. She couldn't remember having been so happy or at peace with herself.

Betsy climbs out from the subway into a splash of sunshine. She no longer feels the dampness of winter and smiles at a woman pushing a stroller along the avenue. Home at last. She quietly lets herself in. The place is silent. The children won't be back from school for another hour. Some adult residents work night shifts and are taking advantage of the calm to sleep before the house resonates with its usual whirlwind of activities.

Betsy tip toes to her room and falls onto the bed. She knows she should get snacks ready for the kids and start on dinner preparations, but her body just wants to be still, if only for a minute. Before she knows it, her eyes close and her mind gives in to the silence.

Then, Carl is there. She thought her husband had died, but here he is, standing next to the bed, accusingly. He wants her to come home and make their daughters respect him again. In the background, Betsy hears a woman's laughter. It has a clear ring, but also a disturbing quality to it, she knows that's the sound she heard that frightful night when she came home from New York, the day her fate took a different turn. Betsy cringes as she tries to hide under the covers. Carl bends towards her and the muffled scream coming out from her heart wakes her.

Betsy's pulse is racing as she tries to ground herself back into reality. "How can I still dream about Carl? The man has been dead five years and he still haunts me."

So much had happened. Ten years ago, she and Mary Beth had settled in Manhattan, one as a housekeeper at La Casa de Maria, a Catholic refuge for individuals or families who found themselves homeless or in crisis, the other with her sister Susan. Soon after, Carl had flown into the city, gone into a rage and attempted to force Betsy back home, to the small Midwestern town where they had both grown up and raised their family. But by that time, Betsy had settled at la Casa, and the atmosphere of joy and hope amid the poverty and sometimes desperation of some the residents had become her own refuge and a chance for finding some peace of mind.

The memory of that fatal night when, returning from New York, she had found another woman in her own bed, would never leave her so she was determined to hold her ground. Carl had then attempted to cajole the girls onto his side but was faced with failure there as well. They had known about their father's ways well before their mother and there was no forgiveness in their heart. At least at that time. He had to fly back home alone and angry. He then twisted the stories so that their son, Carl Junior, would never talk to his mother again and slowly turned the small community that had been Betsy's home for half a century, into a place where she was judged and sentenced but never heard.

Betsy would not divorce her husband. She refused to give in to the threats, strong in her conviction that God meant for what he united not be broken. He eventually gave up but she never received her share of the little they had accumulated over 25 years nor did Carl offer to provide for her or Mary Beth's needs. His drinking escaladed to where he destroyed his liver and his heart gave in. No one cried at the funeral. The redhead Betsy had seen in her room that fateful night had deserted him as soon as the going got rough and he had spent his last few years alone. Even Carl Junior did not grieve, he only hoped that his mother and sisters were out of the will so he would inherit the house. Betsy could have contested the will, but she knew doing so would create more hurt, more resentment so she detached herself from the past sending her son blessings every night in her prayers.

Susan and Mary Beth traveled to their hometown for the funeral. Not, they said, for their father, but hoping to reconnect with their brother. Betsy understood and read between the lines: he was their father regardless of the circumstances. They had loved him as children and this could never be taken away. She watched them go, praying they would find some solace and closure back in the town where they had lived most of their lives. The girls came back broken and with a depth of sadness Betsy had never seen in them. Neighbors and old friends from school, people they had known all their lives turned their backs on them and their brother treated them like strangers. They weren't even allowed to sit in the front pew at the service. Betsy figured that this was the moment when her daughters decided to work hard and prove themselves to those who scorned and humiliated them.

At the time, Mary Beth had completed her graduate studies and armed with an honors doctorate in Psychology, she joined a community clinic. This was where she met Ben who was studying medicine and volunteered at the clinic for extra credits. They started dating and as soon as he began his residency, they got married in a small church ceremony. They struggled for the first few years, but now shared a successful clinic uptown.

Susan's career was still in the restaurant business, but no longer as a server. She was now partner in a small café in Chelsea. No special person in her life but she seemed happy. Betsy smiles remembering Melissa, Susan's old roommate, the first person Betsy had encountered when she arrived in the City. Her name sometimes appeared on playbills, not on the marquis, perhaps, but on Broadway nonetheless.

Calm at last, Betsy looks at the clock by the bed and hears laughter coming from the main gathering room. The kids are back. Time to work.

"Hey, sleeping on the job?" Father Pascal smiles as Betsy rushes through the great room on her way to the kitchen, picking up and tying an apron, one which gives her the look of a giant rhododendron. "I'm just tired lately; maybe when Mary Beth gets a nanny, I'll get more rest." The priest nods in agreement. "You know Betsy, we have a lot of able bodies here right now. You don't have to work so hard. Just think of your family first and we'll pick up the slack." Betsy smiles back, grateful to be working in such an environment.

"Did you ever consider moving in with your daughter?" The priest smiles, "I'm sure she pays more than we do!" Betsy is silent for a second. "No, I don't think that would be a good idea. Their apartment is large, but not large enough for a mother-in-law." The man laughs and nods again, "I understand, and, I must say I'm glad you're staying here. It just wouldn't be the same without you."

Father Pascal always speaks to Betsy in English, but by now, she is fluent in Spanish and the many dialects she has been exposed to over the last decade.

Who would have thought that at her age she could not only start a new job, a new life, but also learn a whole new language and assimilate with people of a totally different culture?

The kitchen is alive with half a dozen children searching for a quick fix before dinner. Betsy has to fight her way to the refrigerator where she removes a carrot shaped container filled with raw vegetables for the kids. She laughs when one inserts two celery sticks in his nose and has the others guess which animal he represents. "Hey, you're going to eat the celery, right?" She says. The kid makes a funny face and to the disgust of others, starts chewing on the sticks."

##

Nine o'clock. Betsy is always grateful for that time of day when everything and everyone wind down for the night. The older children are reading quietly or doing homework while the younger ones sleep. Two of the mothers who are currently down on their luck, are in the living room watching some inane reality show. Lucy joins them. She enjoys listening to the women's comments, looking for ways to reach out and help them in whatever small way she can.

Father Pascal walks in from the evening service. He is shivering as he takes his jacket off and runs for the kitchen. "Tea anyone?" he asks at random. "Sure" one of the women replies. Betsy runs after the priest and insists on making the brew for all of them. She opens the freezer and finds that the small pieces of cake she had squirreled away after one of the children's birthday party are still there. She sets them out on a plate and is ready to head back to the living room when father Pascal stops her.

The priest leads her back to the kitchen. "Betsy," the man starts, "I'm sorry to do this, but there's a special event at the church for the Knights next Saturday, and they need our help to put it together." He looks sheepishly at Betsy. "I told them we could since it'll be a huge fund raiser for us, but I know it's your day off... do you mind? You can take another day the following week. What with Juanita and Maria unemployed, they can take over for you.

Betsy is disappointed. Her birthday is coming up and she had hoped the kids would invite her to a restaurant or something on that Saturday. However, after all Father Pascal had done for her, she can't let him down.

"No problem, Father. You can count on me." She smiles at him and leaves with the tea pot, followed by the priest holding the plate with cake and some cookies the kids have managed to leave behind.

##

The next day, Betsy calls Susan, then Mary Beth just to say hello and tells them she has to work on the following Saturday. They hadn't invited her yet, but she hoped they would show disappointment or make another date with her, but no. Both seem to just acknowledge the information as small talk and go on to talk about their own lives.

Mary Beth is still struggling to find proper day care or a nanny for Alex. She brings him to the clinic, or asks her sister to help when she can get away from her business, but the stress is mounting. Her husband says she is too picky, but Betsy understands how difficult it must be for a mother to leave such a small child in the care of a stranger. She promises to help as much as she can. Nothing special. Then she thinks, why not? "Mary, why don't you bring Alex here? I know it's a long way from home and work, but I'm here all day, we have the facility for babies and there aren't any here right now." Her daughter is silent. "Well," she continues, "what do you think?"

"Did you ask Father Pascal? All he needs is another brat taking up space. Especially when he knows we can afford day care." He mom smiles. "Ah, but maybe you can pay something for his care and help the Casa at the same time." Betsy is amazed at her own insight. "Well, let me talk about it with Ben and I'll call you back."

Betsy hangs up and wonders what the good Father will think. "I'm sure it'll be OK," she tells herself out loud. She'll wait until Mary Beth gives her the go ahead before placing Father Pascal in front of a done deal. Betsy finds this is usually the best way to get things approved and done.

The next day, Mary Beth calls back and agrees to the arrangement. "But know, mom, that it's only temporary. I'll figure something out soon. We'll bring him in Monday morning if it's ok"

Betsy is glad but she now must tell the priest. He is now away visiting a sick parishioner, so she has time to formulate her spiel.

The door bell rings. Unusual for this time of day Betsy thinks. Everyone is usually either working, out job hunting, sleeping, in school or otherwise away. She answers the door, first cautiously, then opens it wide when faced with a young woman, shaking with cold and fear in her colorful woolen jacket. "May I help you?" Betsy offers.

"I hope so." The young woman is slim, too slim. She looks like a critter just out of the sewer. "I," she hesitates, "I have nowhere to go. I've been here a month trying to find a job but..." she lowers her eyes, "I've been living on the street for a while and," she hesitates, "I'm scared." She stopped a moment to compose herself. "Someone told me about La Casa and I thought…" Her eyes were begging. Betsy opens the door and shows her in. "I'm Betsy, what is your name?" Betsy asks. "Francesca."

"Come in Francesca and welcome. I'm sure we can find you some help. Just you sit here and I'll get some hot chocolate." Betsy goes to the kitchen wondering who that woman is. "Not a runaway," she thinks, "maybe just someone in trouble at the wrong time and the wrong place." Betsy thinks. The girl has long black hair, deep green eyes and is not the type of woman she is used to seeing at La Casa. Under the grime, she can tell this girl is different. Maybe it's her accent and the way she carries herself.

Francesca drinks the hot chocolate so quickly that Betsy wonders when was the last time she had a meal. "All right. Now Francesca, you can stay here for dinner and talk to Father Pascal who can figure out what is best for you. Make yourself comfortable and," she smiled, "get ready for the kids to get back to school in half an hour. She sits with this guest for a while, not wanting her to feel out of place, then goes back to the kitchen to start preparing snacks and dinner. She notices the newcomer picking up a magazine from the coffee table rather than turning the television on.

Betsy often loses track of time, but this time, she suddenly realizes it is past four and she hasn't yet heard the usual noises from the kids getting home from school. She rushes to the living room and stops: there, in the middle of the carpet, Francesca is showing the kids how to play some intricate, but fascinating game of cards. They are quietly listening and getting enthusiastic at what they foresee will be the winning outcome.

They all look up when Betsy walks in. "Hey," one boy calls out, "this is amazing. Did you ever play this game Miss Betsy?" Betsy looks at the card displayed on the floor, "I don't think I know this one. Doesn't anyone want a snack?" "After we're done," the kids all say at the same time.

Betsy shrugs and goes back to her pots and pans in the kitchen.

When Father Pascal arrives later, she takes advantage and corners him about Alex. He can read her mind so well. "Betsy, I know you've already arranged it, so why are you asking me?" She blushes. "Well, I can cancel if you want." The priest shakes his head. "Betsy, you've been our house mother here, what? Nine, ten years? You should know by now that your decisions are as good as mine… by the way who is this young woman in the living room?"

"She just showed up at the door this afternoon," Betsy explains "and I told her you'd talk to her and see how we can help. She is totally amazing with the kids. I've never seen them so quiet and focused. I think she actually got them to do their homework before dinner… I say she's a keeper."

Father Pascal laughs then finds Francesca and directs her to his office. After an hour of probing and talking, he is quite impressed with the new arrival. She confessed that she is pregnant and that her parents were so upset, they told her to quit school and started talking about sending her away to live with a relative. She wanted neither but didn't know where to go from there. Her friends or relatives would have taken her back home and she didn't want that, so she took a train to the city where she thought no one would find her and tried to find a job.

"You can stay with us for a while; I think there is a free bed in the girls' room. How old are you, and please be honest." Francesca lowers her eyes, "I'm seventeen. I was going to graduate high school this year." "Well, if you give me your parents' number, I'll make sure they know you're ok, but for now, make yourself at home and we'll see how it goes over the next couple of weeks." Francesca pleads, "Please don't tell them where I am." The man pauses, and asks: "Did you just confess that story to me?" The young woman is taken aback. "Well," she hesitates, "I guess." Father Pascal nods. "Since this was a confession, I can't reveal any of it to anyone. So please give me your permission to call your parents and I'll make sure they leave you be for the time being." He hears a sigh of relief from Francesca as he rises to show the meeting is over and leads her to her new, but crowded, bedroom. "You know you'll have to pull your weight around here and look for a job. Betsy is very strict about that. She'll also nag you about going back to school."

Alex shows up on Monday morning eager and ready to take on a new world. This is his first time in a new environment without his mom since he went home from the hospital. Parents and grandmother are all a little weary, but the baby seems perfectly happy. Betsy marvels at how great her life is. What a blessing it is to love your work and be with people you love all at the same time. A prayer of thanks and joy rises from her heart.

Now alone with the baby, Betsy congratulates herself for such a perfect solution. Yes, they have to travel out of their way to bring him here, but they know he is safe and well taken care of and she gets to hold him and dote on him all day.

Francesca is out looking for work. She walks back in at lunch time, discouraged and on the verge of tears. "Betsy, what will I do?" Then Alex lets out a hungry scream which turns Francesca into a little girl worried about her doll. "What's wrong with him? Let me see." She walks in the nursery and finds the baby needing a change of diaper as well as craving mom's milk. She asks Betsy to warm up the breast milk and announces that she'll personally feed the baby.

Betsy always looks forward to feeding time, but seeing how Francesca has completely forgotten her own problems while taking care of Alex, she lets her take over thinking she will need the practice. God only knows what she'll have to go through once her own baby is born. She shakes her head and starts heating up the milk. She wonders if Francesca has considered an abortion.

As a good Catholic, she always thought that women getting abortions were murdering their children. Now, after ten years of seeing the poverty and hunger where some children are raised, not to mention their often eventual fall into gangs, ending up in jail or dead, she had develop a new sense of right and wrong.

She now believes that every child deserves the right to be wanted, nurtured and loved. Battered women or young runaways living in the streets can barely provide for themselves let alone a child. So, Betsy has reconciled herself with the thought that those women need to have a choice of whether to carry a new person in the often ugly world they live in. She knows in her heart that God loves these women since he understands their burden of pain and weaknesses. She has strong reservations about the fathers of these children, however, and suspects they will go straight down the burning way.

The next morning, Francesca finds herself with a bout of morning sickness and stays home, earning her keep, she says, by taking care of Alex. Mary Beth is now convinced that this arrangement, while inconvenient, is allowing her to concentrate on her patients without fear of whether her child's caretaker is adequate or not. Her husband Ben, however, is finding the five AM rising and the trek to La Casa at rush hour with a baby to be stressing. He has always let Mary Beth figure the household matters out, including those to do with Alex, but now, he has to be involved and is not sure it is working out for him. He has to admit, however, that every night he has picked up his child from La Casa, Alex looks happier and healthier than ever. But Ben is tired.

The week goes by and Betsy is ready for the Saturday event. She's not sure what it consists of, but she knows there will be food, drinks, hence a lot for her to help with. She is told it is a dress up affair so she should wear her best dress, even if she has to wear an apron on top of it.

She gets up early and walks to the church, going down the stairs to the basement which serves as a parish hall, to see what preparations need be done. She sees the tables and chairs are already set up, so she completes the task with tablecloths, utensils, napkins and trays for the buffet table. That's when father Pascal arrives and tells her she can go, but that she should come back at around six, just before everyone gets there, to help with the food and serving. She goes back to La Casa and takes a well deserved nap.

At four, she showers, taking a bit more time than usual with her hair and decides on a black skirt and top Susan gave her last Christmas. Armed with her favorite white apron ironed to a crisp and a pair of comfortable shoes to change into once no one notices her anymore, she puts her coat on and walks back to the hall.

The room is still quite dark so she assumes they are waiting until people arrive before turning the lights on to save on the electric bill. She takes her coat off, hangs it on a hook at the bottom of the stairs, walks in and all the lights come shining on her. She's not sure if she's having a dream, a heart attack or both.

Everyone is there singing Happy Birthday and one of the tables she set up is filled with wrapped boxes. She just stands there, stunned, still not understanding what is happening.

Susan is the first to come and give her a hug. "Happy birthday mom." Betsy is still stunned. "Hey,

Mom, are you OK?" Betsy nods, but is still muted by the surprise. Mary Beth comes over. "Happy birthday, Mom. We're so glad you're our mom!" By now Betsy has tears in her eyes and doesn't know what to do next. She just stands there. Ben comes over, holding Alex in his arms and together with Father Pascal they bring Betsy to the head table where fresh flowers cover the center and crystal glasses, brought in especially for the guest of honor, gleam under the bright lights.

She looks around and sees what looks like hundreds of people in the hall, but she knows she must be wrong. She doesn't know anyone much in the city. Then she looks closely: seems like all the woman, men and children she has taken care of over the last ten years are there. How hard must have this been to put together? She wonders. Her eyes, now blinded by tears, can no longer distinguished one person from another. They are all one as they are in her heart.

Someone starts playing the piano, a soft ballad, and she begins receiving wishes from all the people she had learned to love but whom she thought had forever left her life to finally live their own.

The women currently staying at La Casa are the ones doing the serving and helping. Betsy is the star. She smiles through her tears. How far can one go in ten years? As far as the moon and sun. Now she knows that.

Everyone settles down at a table and the food appears like magic on the buffet. Someone prepares a plate of food for the guest of honor and presents it to her. Betsy tries to remember if she has ever been served that way, and can't say that she ever has. This is too much. She feels love out of the passionate conversations all her friends are having. "This is what heaven must be like." She thinks to herself and then says to her daughters who have joined her at the table. Once everyone has filled their plates at the colorful buffet table, Father Pascal rises to say grace, adds a few words of affection for the guest of honor and everyone starts enjoying the home made feast of Mexican delicacies.

After dinner, people come to the microphone to tell of experiences they had with Betsy. She is stunned. She believed all this time that the tiny things she did for people may gain her a few brownie points towards heaven, but she never realized how much they meant to the ones she did them for. She is tonight's star but feels humbled at the same time.

Then the time comes to open the gifts. Most presents are handmade: scarves, winter socks, painted Madonna's or crosses, jewelry crafted from beads or other found items. The best gifts she has ever received. As soon as guests start dancing to music closer to salsa, Mary Beth and Susan walk over and hand her an envelope. Ben follows with Alex back in his arms. They are all smiles.

"I don't want anything, please I don't need anything. This is one of the best days of my life, nothing more can make me happier than I am." "Come on mom, just open it."

She opens the envelope and in it, is a letter from Father Pascal giving her a forced two week vacation, and, he wrote, whether she likes it or not. The other document is a travel voucher for a trip to the tropics. Two weeks in paradise, it says on the brochure.

"What?" she says, not quite understanding, "What is that?" "Mom, we're throwing you out! You're going away to get some well deserved R & R on the most magnificent beach in the world." "But I can't do that. I have responsibilities. Besides, I just wouldn't fit in with all the pretty people down there."

"No, mom. You're going." Susan said. "We checked it out and this is not a commercial place. The hotel is tiny and we heard a nice woman runs it, so no ifs or buts... you're going and that's final. We'll all manage without you. I even told Mary Beth I would take some time off myself to help out at La Casa with Alex."

As if the ground below her is slipping away, Betsy feels her legs weaken and sits back in the chair. She quickly looks up to reassure everyone, smiles, and then puts her arms out for Alex while motioning her children to join the festivities on the dance floor.

##

CLARA

P acking again. Seems like I do a lot of that lately. This time, though, it's different: I'm retiring. The only therapy I want to provide anymore is to some chickens or cows out in the field. Over ten years in the big city and I'm ready to be put to pasture... literally. I've had enough. I've heard every problem conceivable from my patients and I can't take it anymore, but first, there is something I have to do.

Well, honestly? I can't seem to enjoy life in New York now that Clara has left. In fact, her story is one that should be heard and retold to women everywhere. No, she is still alive, but chose to join her daughter in London last year, giving up on the city she had loved so much.

As I read my last notes about her condition almost ten years ago, tears start welling in my eyes. I remember how, in spite of her cancer, the chemo and her failing knees, she kept her chin up and a smile on her face. Her optimism was unfortunately not rewarded by the fate that led the following years. I didn't chronicle the events of those years for fear that my words may injure her soul, should she run across them, but now I feel I owe it to other women to document this phase of her life.

##

"Hey," Clara shouted at me, "are you daydreaming or what?" I turned my head and smiled. Clara was in remission now. It had been two years since her cancer was diagnosed and her hair had stubbornly refused to grow more than a few curled, weak, baby-like, but steel colored duvet. She wore a colorful scarf, island-style, one which made her perfect dark skin glow in this early spring light. She had refused to wear a wig from the beginning and was not about to start now. "Yes," I replied, "I was imagining the both of us on a beach somewhere, you in a bikini, looking sharp and me in a muumuu eying the local colors."

Clara laughed. "Sounds great, except for the fact that I have no money, I'm in debt over my head and... a Bikini? I don't think so." I had to tell her. She looked great no matter what or how little or what colors she wore. "Besides," she added, "I think I'm persona non grata when it comes to vacations these days. After all the time off I had for my problem, I may have to die first!" She never referred to her cancer as more than 'my issue', 'my problem' or, my favorite, 'this fucking annoying thing that happened'.

We were sitting on a park bench in Washington Square. It was spring and kids were in high gear warm weather mode, playing hard and loud, shedding scarves, hats and coats along the way. There was a sense of 'life coming home again' in the air and Clara sensed it too. "I'll be all right." She said, reading my thoughts. "I know." She took a joint out of her bag and discreetly started to smoke. "I thought you said you'd quit after you got better." I chided her. She shrugged and smiled. "Yeah, I said that, but I thought about it and decided not to."

She then turned to me, all excited. "Did I tell you I met this guy last week?" She had not and I looked up, waiting to hear more. "He was at my neighbor's house-warming party last week. Oh, did I tell you, I have a new neighbor. Her name is Charlotte and she's about our age. I think she said she works at the bank, you know the one near the supermarket? Anyway, she's a little fat if you want to know and totally unkempt. But, she seems like she has a lot of nice friends."

I was getting impatient. "What about this guy," I asked trying to steer her back to the initial conversation. "Oh yeah, sorry," she took a puff and giggled, "he's kind of cute, for an over fifty dude. Not too tall and just enough gray in his hair to make him look distinguished and not too much fat around the middle, if you know what I mean." She winked. "And, most importantly, he gave me 'the look'." I had to inquire as to the nature of the look. She laughed. "The flirting kind. He asked me out and I think I'll say yes." She shuffled in her bag with her free hand and put a torn piece of paper with a number under my nose. "He even gave me his number. What do you think?" I turned to look at her and couldn't help shaking my head. "What do you know about this guy?"

"Well, she started, he's cute, as I was saying, and I think he's German or something like that, but he doesn't have an accent. I'm not sure what he does, but he was nicely dressed and, well, I can't be picky these days anyway." Her laughter was light and seemed to fit in well with the day. I asked her to let me know about the date and not to leave anything out. I was amazed to note that her normal cynicism was completely absent from her tone and reflected at how men should not have the power to transform perfectly good, cynical women into giddy teenagers. I didn't share this insight with Clara. I was glad to see her in such a happy frame of mind.

We left the park, Clara, still smiling, trying to hide the joint pain shooting from her knee that even the 'magical' herb couldn't mask, and me pretending not to notice.

We were to meet for happy hour and a play the following week, but she called to cancel, telling me that her date a few days earlier had been 'awesome' and that she was going out again on the night we had planned our own outing. I tried to be supportive, but I confess I was quite disappointed.

As an aside, I always wondered why women often dump girlfriends the minute a man pays attention to them. Younger women tell me it is a generational thing: apparently, my generation of women was brought up to always look at men for validation and drop everything for them, whereas the new wave of girls supposedly strives for independence. I don't buy it. Every time I see young women wearing ten inch heels and low cut shirts carrying designer brief cases, or a girl wearing a princess outfit or pushing a doll carriage, every time I chance upon the disgustingly pink aisle in a toy store, I suspect the marketing folks aren't ready to promote independence for women yet.

It pains me that for all the independence and freedom we worked so hard for, women, even Clara, still fall back to the old submissive ways.

It was another two weeks before I saw Clara again. She was beaming. Claus, that was her new beau's name, was fantastic: he was kind, sensitive and knew how to make her feel good, which had been a rare commodity over the last few months. Her knee pain had become more serious and she received steroid shots so she could ignore it a bit longer. In some way, it was good to see her acting like a young girl overwhelmed by a first love. I was glad for her, but sad to see our friendship waning in the wake of this amorous tide. She kept looking at her watch and when I asked if she had other plans, she hesitated and admitted that Claus called every night at nine thirty and she didn't want to miss his call. I guessed our late nights of wine and commiseration were over, at least for now.

Two months later, she asked me for dinner to introduce the man who was soon to move in with her in Brooklyn since, apparently, his studio in the city was a one person flat. Claus was probably a little younger than I imagined, but these days, who knows? His hair was as Clara had described but with a bit of contrived highlights for dramatic effect and no sign of receding hairline or thinning anytime soon. His fair unblemished skin was remarkable and the matching blue eyes were protected by long curly lashes only women should be allowed to have. He wasn't much taller than Clara, but his proportional figure was nice to look at. I could see why my friend had been smitten by this man.

Apart from his physical appearance, my first impression was not one I would share with Clara. The man's conversation was shallow, often offering irrelevant or off topic comments on the subjects Clara and I were discussing. I found it unnerving how his eyes shifted from one thing to another, never making eye contact with me, even as I addressed him directly. To his credit, I noted how protective he was of Clara, defending her point of view regardless of the issue; or was it possessive? It's often hard to distinguish between the two. I was really uncomfortable as a third wheel with this man my friend was obviously completely enthralled with. I suspected that she was transferring all her will to live to Claus who, against all odds in her own mind, was in love with her. If one can rebound from cancer, this was what it appeared to me and I couldn't see it lasting.

I didn't find out much about him except that he was an insurance man who worked in a small agency in the city and, until next month, lived in a walk-up studio in Little Italy. He was a smooth talker. I was really trying to silence the voices in my head which told me to refuse any offer of friendship he may have.

Over the following two years, I all but lost touch with Clara. I would meet her for lunch every couple of months, but the friendship had lost its gloss. Now that she was in long term remission, she had decided to get the knee surgery her orthopedist had suggested. At least I knew she could finally walk without pain. Claus was still around and after the first few months of glee, Clara no longer talked about him.

"How's Claus?" I asked at one of our encounters. "Fine." Her evasive answer told me not to pursue the subject so I moved on to our now usual inane banter or discussions on new styles, the weather or how the country was going down the tube. We had lost the connection. She had started wearing a wig.

I also noticed she was getting thinner. I worried at how little she ate when we met for lunch. When I mentioned it to her, she just looked down at her food. "Well, I'm not a young chick anymore and I have to stay thin if I want to keep my man." She giggled in an unconvincing way and quickly changed the subject.

A few days before Christmas about four years ago, I answered a call from her just as I was getting ready for bed. "Hey," she started, "I had a bit of an accident." She stopped. I panicked. "Are you OK?" I frantically asked. "Yeah, I'm OK, I guess, but can you come over?" I could tell from the sound of her voice that she didn't want me to question her request. She just wanted me there. "Of course. Just tell me where you are and I'll be right there."

I took a taxi to the emergency room where she was calling from, wondering how bad and what kind of accident she had been a victim of. Knowing my way around the hospital, I passed through security and found her sitting in a cubicle of the emergency room. Her arm was in a cast and she had bruises on her face and neck, I almost lost my cool. I took a deep breath. "What happened?" I asked, but not leaving her time to answer, I let her know that it had to be the truth. No lies, no excuses. "I've been your friend for many years," I also pointed out "and it's not because you've been avoiding me the last while that you can ignore that fact."

Her eyes were riveted to the floor as she was mentally assessing her own situation and how she could relate it to me. Tears were quietly crawling down her cheeks. I knew I had to let her come to me on her own terms. Trying to avoid any sensitive area, I came closer and hugged her the best way I could. Her head fell on my shoulder and the tears turned into a torrent of sobs and words I couldn't understand.

We were in this awkward embrace for some time before she gently eased me away and looked me in the eyes. "I'm sorry." She said. I let her know there was nothing to be sorry about and all I wanted was for her to be well. "It's not fair," she cried, "Why are you there for me every time I have a problem? You should just let me screw up my life and ignore me. It's not fair." All I could reply was that old cliché about how life is never fair and, again, let her gather her thoughts. There was an unusual gleam in her eyes. Her speech was slurred. I lifted her chin to get a closer look. Her pupils were dilated beyond what one would expect from just smoking marijuana. "What drug are you on?" I asked. But before she could respond, her doctor came in the room with forms to sign. He looked at me, wondering who I was and what I was doing to Clara. My first thought was that I may be a big woman, but I would never hurt a flea. I put my hand out and introduced myself both as a psychologist and Clara's friend. I felt a twinge in my heart: I wanted to say 'best friend' but found that I couldn't claim that title anymore. Not after the last few years.

"Your friend has sustained multiple injuries and, as you have probably surmised, not as a result of a car accident. I suspect she ran into someone's fist." He was glaring at Clara. "Can you tell me whose that would be?"

I looked at Clara looking for an answer but she just lowered her eyes and bit her lips. "I haven't seen Clara in a while," I confessed, "but I'll find out who did this," Clara raised her head in defiance but I continued, "and I assure you I'll see the man in hell if that's what it takes to stop him." Clara was now trying to hush me down but her doctor told me that while the officer who had found my friend lying down in front of her apartment couldn't get any information out of her, he would personally follow up and make sure this would not happen again.

I knew from experience that when a woman ends up in such a state, it is not a first time occurrence. It is sometimes a slow but sure progressive behavior pattern. "Let me speak to my friend for while." I asked. "Well," the doctor replied, "she has a concussion, so we are admitting her for observation overnight. I'll be back when she is settled in a room. I should tell you, we're also running some drug tests." I could only nod as I watched him leave.

With no one to run interference, I now had a free hand at unlocking the truth. But not yet.

An orderly came in with a gurney, helped her onto it and led us to the third floor and a room already occupied by three other women. It was late however, and all seem to be sleeping, likely with help from the latest fad in hospital sleeping aids.

I stood by while Clara was helped into the bed. "The nurse will be back to check on you soon." He said before closing the curtains around the bed and leaving the room.

"Is it ok if I sit on the edge of the bed?" I asked, afraid to be intrusive, but determined to stay. She shrugged. "Do you mind if I put my 'psych' hat on? It might help you forget who I am." I suggested. She slowly turned her head and cringed at a pain she had forgotten to take into account. "Whatever. I'm sorry."

"First," I told her, "you have to stop apologizing. It's not as though it's your fault." I paused to give her time to digest this. "How do you feel now?" I asked. "Fuck, I'm sore as hell. I feel stupid. I feel I should have died from the cancer." She had used the dreaded C word. "My whole life has been a series of stupid decisions and bad ideas." This was a statement, not a lure to catch some encouragement or denial of her state. I just sat and listened. "Don't lie to me," she continued, "you knew who Claus was the minute you saw him." She glanced up but didn't give me time to respond. "Why didn't you warn me?" I knew this was a rhetorical question. Clara knew well enough that in her state of love euphoria, it would have been futile to contradict her actions. I just remained quiet.

"OK. I guess he was all right at first, only he didn't like it when I hung out with you." She was still looking at me to see a reaction, but I just nodded. "He said you were a dike and people like you are no good to anyone." She paused. "Although he didn't like any of my other friends either." She stopped to gather her thoughts, not expecting anything but for me to listen. "I really loved him, you know. I really thought this was real. I guess, because of my all my bad relationships, I thought only black men were smooth then dumped on you or just dumped you." I had to chime in that time. "Clara, I have had many women walk in my office, most white, some housewives, many lawyers or Wall Street wizards and I can assure you that men like that exist in every class of society and no race or culture can claim a better average than another." I paused. "Now, tell me what happened."

Her story was one I had heard before, one that many women who have never known abuse don't understand. "Why don't they just leave?" is the most common reaction to domestic violence. Well, it doesn't work that way. Many women find themselves in such relationships with a subconscious wish to punish themselves for past mistakes. Men like Claus can sense this and manipulate the woman accordingly. In some cases, a woman, previously abused as a child, finds her comfort zone in such a man: the expected and the known are comforting even when it hurts. This is the most difficult part of the abuse: a young girl's abuser is often the person who appears to love her the most and the child can start enjoying the attention, even the abuse. When she seeks a mate in her teen years, she is more likely to choose a man with similar traits to her former abuser. That has become her comfort zone.

With Clara, cancer had taken a far greater toll on her self-image than she would ever admit to. Having this handsome man desire her and make her feel whole again, was something she couldn't resist and she was blind to any of the telltale signs. Her independence and cynicism had died as the chemo dripped down into her veins. I really should have known that her optimism was for my benefit but I was too close to see it. I genuinely thought she would be fine. My love for Clara had literally blinded me and, in a way, made me an accomplice to what I was witnessing now.

The sequence of events often goes like this: First the man dotes on his girlfriend. Then there may be a small 'incident' but she explains it away and keeps faith in the man who appears to love her so much. He takes her out everywhere she wants to go, almost every night, so the only time she has for other friends or family is lunch. Even a drink after work can't be worked in since she is expected to be home and have a drink with her man. He is always the romantic one and often turns off the phone at night so their intimacy can't be disturbed. Then, there are the flowers after every verbal fight. One day he hits her, but apologizes, he even cries: she went too far is what he says and he just 'lost' it. She consoles him.

Later, the romance dies and he doesn't bother coming up with excuses for berating or hitting her anymore: the woman gets convinced that she deserves the abuse. It just becomes a way of life. In Clara's case, her love of the weed helped him introduce new pain relievers in her life and I suspected that she was now likely addicted to some much stronger chemical or pill.

That was it in a nutshell. Since the police had not found her at home and Claus claimed she was mugged on the sidewalk, their hands were tied and they could do nothing. Of course, Clara remained silent, reminding me that her confession was with me as a doctor, not a friend.

I was beside myself and found my way to her apartment shortly after she was released from the hospital. Clara's arm was still in a cast. The bruises were turning yellow. The way she greeted me, I could tell she was in a place where I couldn't reach her. I chose to confront Claus.

"What the fuck are you doing here?" He spitted out. I could no longer hold back. "I wish I was here to kill you, but don't worry I don't have it in me. All I want you to do is get out of here and not come back."

He laughed and shook his head. "You don't know, do you?" I kept my eyes focused on his face, trying to read what was behind the surface. "I'm not going anywhere. We're married. This is my place and," he pointed to the furniture, "this is my stuff. Hey, she's lucky; I let her quit her job when we got married.

I was flabbergasted. Clara had never told me she had married the bastard let alone quit her job. I sat next to her on the couch trying to digest these facts. Claus poured himself a drink. "To my beautiful bride." Clara smiled. "She needs to get off whatever it is you got her on." He shrugged. "I never got her on anything she wasn't already on. She doesn't want to anyway. Excuse me." I was stunned by his candor and self-assurance.

He left the room and the sounds indicated he was using the bathroom. I got up and ambled around the apartment, wondering what my next move should be. There was a desk next to the couch completely filled with papers obviously linked to his insurance business.

The apartment had the appearance of a place where people slept and ate, maybe sometimes worked, but were very little else was going on, except the occasional domestic dramas. The personal touches and pictures were gone which brought her to wonder what Clara's kids thought about all this.

"Clara," I asked, "have you seen or heard from Louisa or Marco lately?" A daughter in England and a son in California didn't provide any strong family support. She slowly and apparently painfully lifted her head and looked up. "You know, "she slurred, trying to keep her eyes focused," Louisa came over," she hesitated, "I think it was last month. Anyway, she couldn't stay here 'cause well," she makes a weak gesture with her uninjured arm, "it's too crowded, but we had a nice visit. She looked upset. I'm not sure why. Maybe because I forgot to tell her about Claus. I didn't think she'd care. Anyway, I didn't have much time to see her. She's gone now. She hasn't called me lately. I wonder why."

"How about Marco?" "Well, he's still in" she stopped to remember, "California, I think, as far as I know. I've not heard from him over the last while." Her head rolled back onto the couch and she stared at the ceiling as if it would tell her where her son was.

"Have you been going for your tests?" I asked. "Tests?" "Yes, remember you had cancer. You have to be tested regularly." She looked at me. "Well, I don't remember. I did see a doctor after we got married. Oh," she laughed "by the way, Claus and I are married now. Weird hey? Anyway I sort of got some tests but, I don't know, more like ordinary test stuff." She giggled again. "Claus was mad 'cause I smoked a joint before the first appointment." She laughed. "We had to go back home and make another date. He was really mad and threw all my stuff away." I asked her if it was how she ended up in the hospital, but she didn't answer. In her fog, she continued "Actually, it's funny because Claus had to keep me off the weed for a while. He didn't want the test to show any drugs." She laughed. "Too late for that now."

The man was now back in the room and I could think of nothing more I could accomplish that night. I whispered to Clara to call me anytime day and night if she needed me and slipped my card in her jacket pocket. She nodded absentmindedly.

Over the next few weeks, I looked for an address or an email where I could contact her kids and sent them a calm but concerned letter which I was hoping would get them to intervene. I also contacted her oncologist who told me he hadn't heard from Clara for years now. Maybe she had a new one, but further research didn't indicate a new doctor or any doctor at all. I took it upon myself to make an appointment for her to be tested, and called her that night. Claus answered the phone and said Clara was asleep.

I cancelled all my appointments for the next day and went over to Brooklyn, waited across the street until I saw Claus leave for work and rang the door bell. After getting no answer, I slipped in behind another tenant, walked up to her floor and started banging on the door for what seemed like an eternity. Clara finally came to the door. "Where's the fire?" She then noticed it was me standing in the corridor, backed off and left the door open. I walked in the apartment which appeared in more disarray than I remembered from only a short while ago. I told her about the appointment but she said Claus said she wasn't insured anymore and couldn't see a doctor. "That's nonsense. He works in insurance." I almost screamed at her. "Just don't tell him. I'll pay for it if I have to. Clara you're family to me I need you to do this for me. Please come next week and don't mention it to Claus, please." I begged.

She shrugged and crashed on the couch. "I guess I've been feeling pretty crummy lately. But what if he finds out I've been out?" I told her I'd deal with it, still with murderous thoughts, but trying to stay calm for her sake. I intended to see her doctor prior to the appointment to bring him up to date on Clara's health and situation. When I met with him, we both agreed that if her children responded, we would compel her to seek treatment for the drugs and, we hoped, a divorce from Claus. I know this is unusual for a specialist to be involved that way, but my ties with the medical profession helped. I often got referrals from oncologists and these connections open doors when I need a favor.

The following week, I squirreled Clara away from her apartment and we took a cab to the hospital where her doctor had ordered a battery of tests. The wait was long and Clara was getting impatient, knowing that if Claus found out about this, he would be furious. I tried to ask why he would be so angry, but, first, she didn't want to talk about it, and second, I knew the answer. This was typical of men who wanted ultimate control over their mate. She made me promise to keep this visit between ourselves. When the rounds of tests were completed, I made an appointment for her to come back the following week for results. Clara heard and panicked. "I can't do this again next week. No, I can't. Sorry." And she ran out before I could catch up to her.

I couldn't believe what had happened to my friend. Sadly, I know this can happen to anyone, given the right (or wrong) circumstances and that, in itself, is very scary.

##

It was after midnight. I was already in bed when the phone rang. This time a man was on the phone. It was a week since Clara and I had been to the hospital for tests and I was trying to think of a way to take her back for the results and consultation.

The man politely and calmly asked if I could come down to the emergency room. An ambulance had brought someone in, but they couldn't identify her. The person had my business card in her pocket and he hoped I could help. I dressed as quickly as I could, trying not to let my imagination wander. It took a few minutes to get a taxi so I pressed the driver to get there as fast as he could. I admit I was hoping it would be one of my patients, but deep inside I knew who was lying in the hospital at the end of the cab ride. It was pouring rain and the traffic was slow. I was in agony.

My fears were justified. Clara was hardly recognizable, blood all over her face, bandages attempting to hide the wounds, her body broken. She was lying on a gurney, unconscious. I cried. The police officer who had responded to an anonymous call came up and gently tapped my shoulder. "I'm sorry Ma'am, but we need to know the woman's identity." I lifted my head and faced a round faced woman in uniform who was obviously very uncomfortable with the situation. I nodded and gave her Clara's name.

"Did you arrest Claus?" I asked. "There was no one else on the street when we arrived. The man who called didn't identify himself. A good thing we got there when we did. A few minutes later and she might have bled out. Do you have any idea who could have done that? We thought it was a mugging or rape gone wrong." I had to take a deep breath. "Look for her husband." I gave the officer the address of the apartment, with the assurance that the man was guilty and urging her to make an arrest. She backed off, thanked me and left.

I was stunned. I should have known. I should have done something. Guilt was eating me up. Then there was a moan. I rushed over to her side and touched her shoulder where there seemed to be no wounds or bruises. She cringed from my touch, and then tried to open her swelled eyes with no success. "It's ok, it's me. I'm here, Clara. I'm here and it's over. I will never leave your side if I have to crazy glue myself to you." I think she tried to smile, but the cut lip made her face turn into a painful mask. "Shhh," I urged her to stay relaxed and calm. I bent to kiss her temple. "I'll take care of everything. Don't you worry. I'm here." I had no idea of what to do, but I was there and determined to stay.

I knew cell phones were not allowed in the hospital, but I didn't care. I immediately sent text messages to Louisa and Marco to come over STAT.

There was no more negotiating or procrastinating. Clara needed her family around her. I needed them to help me help Clara.

The emergency room was busy: a full moon, I was told by the nurse checking on my friend. I'm not sure I believe that more injuries and accidents happen on such nights, but I have often been told by other medical professionals that they consider it a fact of life. All I could do was wait. Wait and hope. I hadn't done so in a long time, but I found myself praying. Not to any one particular God or spirit but just praying. My mind needed to retreat to a place where there is love, peace and serenity and the God of my childhood who abases women, encourages hate and war while causing children to suffer and die as a test of their parents' faith, didn't work for me, especially in times like this.

My meditation was ended by the nurse who came in to check Clara's vital signs. "Is she going to be ok?" I asked. The nurse hesitated, shrugged and told me it was touch and go. They wanted to operate as they suspected internal bleeding, but she was not stable enough to go under the knife yet. I nodded as she was injecting more pain medication in the IV and making sure the wounds were clotting under the bandages. She smiled at me and left.

##

From that day came weeks of hardship for Clara who finally had to concede and give Claus up to the authorities. Her children had come the very next day and stayed with her until she was deemed on the way to recovery. Old drugs were leaving her system as new ones were entering it. She was in constant pain but numbed by a much deeper soul wound.

I had to wait over a month before finding out what had happened that fated night. The telephone was ringing just as Claus walked in the apartment. He rushed past Clara to answer and when he told the oncologist's administrative assistant that Clara was unavailable, she asked Claus to remind his wife of the next day's appointment. He had been duped. He promptly grabbed her by her shirt and demanded to know what was going on. She was high, maybe higher than usual, so she just blew him off, sending him in a furious rage. Clara was a rag doll which he hit and kicked until he thought she was dead. Then he panicked, threw her down the stairs and laid her on the sidewalk before he made the 911 call from a pay phone. He then apparently started concocting a story on what happened and eventually returned to the apartment to clean up and pretend he was in bed the whole time. But this time it didn't work. The authorities were there before he had a chance to completely obliterate his crime. There was still enough evidence in the apartment to send him away for a long time.

The guilt was eating me. It was really all my fault. When is it ok to cross the line of respect for other's decisions? I know I had no legal way to force Clara into leaving Claus or quitting drugs, but what about my moral obligations? I should have been stronger even if it meant bullying her into it. As it were, I took a leave of absence to help my friend, but also to work out my own debilitating issues.

A few days before she was released, after spending two months in the hospital and another three months in a rehab facility for physical therapy and drug treatment, I went to her apartment wanting to erase any traces that Claus had ever lived there. I had made sure the rent was paid so she wouldn't be homeless after she healed. I cleaned and even had the kitchen and living room painted in an attempt to bring her home back to the way it was when I first visited her years ago. I also found old family pictures in boxes piled high in a closet, bought new frames and displayed those memories of more cheerful times around the apartment.

As I was clearing Claus' desk, I chanced upon an insurance policy on Clara's life for half a million dollars with Claus as beneficiary. My anger was so strong, I had to sit and regain some composure before continuing my task. As soon as I was done, I brought the documents to a lawyer friend to be sure this would be included in the case against Claus. As for the policy,

I personally saw to it that it got cancelled and the premium refunded to Clara.

Clara's children came again, this time with their own children, to celebrate Clara's return home. She was so moved, she couldn't stop crying. As I had promised her, I made arrangements to stay at her place until I felt I was no longer needed.

I filled out the forms for her disability benefits so she could remain independent and urged her to file a civil suit against Claus to make sure he would have nothing left should he ever be released from prison. I was still with her a few months later when new cancer tests proved positive. The beast was back.

This felt like a 'do-over', a distorted rerun of a bad show. There was no joking this time, no play. Clara let herself be cared for without complaints. She had lost her spirit. In spite of years of addressing other's concerns, I was at a complete loss with my friend. I didn't know what to do, so I just decided to be there and let her heal in her own time. On top of it all was her having to testify against her husband, the subsequent divorce and all that encompassed. Life was not kind to such a gentle woman. The settlement from the civil suit would never compensate for what she had suffered at this man's hand.

Once the new cycle of treatments was over, the nausea a thing of the past and the hair budding again on her beautiful head, I still remained with her, leaving early for work and rushing back to be sure all was well in the afternoon. She remained on track this time. She didn't have the will to wish for anything except perhaps a swift death, which was what I was there to prevent.

Time heals everything they say. Maybe. Clara did get better, but the old Clara was gone forever. We no longer 'hung out' at happy hour. Her bout with drug addiction had put her in a very fragile state and she feared being around anyone that may be, or even appear to be high. We just had coffee at her table or mine, sometimes at a local sidewalk café, but never in a bar.

I have been packing my books lately but today I am filling a suitcase with summer clothes. Clara and I are meeting on a beach, to celebrate her 60 years of life. The resort is way down south where no one can find us. Being alive is the important part, but our being together is the most special thing to me. She'll never know this, and I'll never tell her, but Clara is the love of my life. I knew it was never to be, so I kept this part of myself hidden so she would trust me no matter what.

She never suspected and I will never let her know. The place I chose is called: "My Last Dream".

Hers may be fulfilled one day, but mine never will be. I have crossed that dream line a couple of years ago, the line where everything is no longer possible and new beginnings are rare and elusive. I have now reconciled myself to growing old alone but with no regrets.

##

PATRICIA

The back door won't budge. "Damn," Patricia thought, "I thought the snow season was finally over." An overnight storm had covered the ground with a heavy coat of white fluff, just as she thought the old dirty stuff was finally melting. Yesterday's wet ground cover below the new snow had frozen and held the door hostage. Finally she pushed it with her hip and shoulder as she has seen people do it on cop shows and the door opened at last. A frigid gust of wind sent her back inside, wet and frustrated. The hens were well taken care of by a neighboring farmer, but this morning she had such a craving for warm, freshly laid eggs, that she had decided to go out and get her own from the coop. But the blustering wind mixed with the white mushy mess in the yard told her that there was no picking of fresh eggs for her this morning.

Patricia sighed, poured herself another cup of coffee and resolved to keep activities, especially outdoor ones, to a minimum today.

She poured sugar, then milk in the dark brew and fondly thought about the mud she had to navigate through the day she came back to her childhood home almost ten years ago. The thousand mile trek that had finally brought her to the home she had grown up in. The trip that had her saying goodbye to a life she had cherished but one she knew was over after Bill died.

100

The memory of her husband brought tears to her eyes. It always did. In spite of all that happened before and after their life together, the years with this man were the most precious to her.

She looked around the kitchen, remembering how she had managed to live in this house while working to bring it to the point of being inhabitable comfortably and also legally. She smiled, convinced that it should have been condemned at the time. But, all things considered, she had done well.

In the hall, the walls were covered with paper, similar to the one her mother had hung before she died when Patricia was still a child. This was not a trendy renovation. This was the restoration of a past that had happened long ago and held fond memories this woman wanted to cling to. She had erased all traces of her sister, except for a photograph that showed the two of them together with their mother in better times, before Patricia had to leave her home, abandoned and hurt. She never found a picture of her father and that was fine with her.

"Sixty," she thought, "I'll be sixty." She shook her head in disbelief and wondered how the last ten years had gone by so fast. Selling the house she had shared out east with Bill was the hardest thing she had to do. All she had kept was his favorite recliner and a box of cards and knick knacks he had given to her on birthdays or anniversaries over the years. Everything else in this renovated house was old fashioned, but new except for the dining room set. Some would call the remodel 'retro', she just called it home.

Patricia stood up and walked through the dining room. Her grandmother's table was its center piece with a matching sideboard along the wall. These were the only things she had salvaged from the original farm house. When she was growing up, no one was allowed to eat or do homework on the rosewood table, but now, she spent many hours in this room, using its refinished table as often as she could, regardless of how seldom she entertained.

Restoration had been a challenge. Water leaking from the floor above had left it damaged and rotting, some had said beyond repair. But she had found the right craftsman and there it was, looking just as it did when she was a girl when no one was allowed to touch any of the shiny, polished wood.

Now seated in the living room, Patricia wondered how she managed to continue living after Bill died. They were enough for each other. She wondered if, had he lived to a ripe old age, they would have been this couple who, when one partner dies, the other follows soon after.

She and Bill were each other's best friend. They were soul mates and needed no other relationships. When she moved to her childhood home it was without help or support. She had no old friends in this town either. Most of her high school classmates had moved on to larger cities. The ones who didn't had followed in their parents' footsteps as farmers or taken over the family business. She fortunately had never crossed paths with the boy whose cruelty had caused her to shun this town for good. She never was interested in finding out where he was, even after going to college and having access to all the legal documents she would have needed to do so.

"God, I can't believe I did this." She thought about the years spent at the local branch of the state university getting a law degree she wasn't even sure she wanted. With many years working as a legal assistant, the transition was not too painful. Bill was also a lawyer, not a famous or even a good one, but he left her with a comfortable sum. The marital house, sold at the height of market, had easily paid for all the renovations to the farmhouse.

After graduation, Patricia joined the district attorney's office at first, then moved on to become a court appointed defense lawyer, catering to the poor, the disfranchised and, unfortunately, the felons and perverts. Last year she had reduced her hours by half and begun to volunteer as a Guardian ad Litem for children facing criminal charges. She found this rewarding and depressing at the same time, but it made the time fly and this is what she liked best about these endless activities.

Lately, she was experiencing anxiety attacks. Her office mate noticed the occasional discomfort and suggested she may be burning out: "There is only so much you can do for people, you know," the woman had claimed, "sometimes, they're just rotten and there is nothing you or me can do about it." Patricia didn't believe that, but, regardless, she didn't think work was the cause of her stress.

She had sensed a black cloud descending upon her for a while. She even had checked with a doctor to rule out any physical reasons for what ailed her. No, it was something else. Something missing. She wondered if turning sixty this year was a factor. In these modern times, she could probably work forever, so retirement was not something she even thought about, but going to the office, the court room and back home every day for perhaps 40 years? This was something to think about.

Patricia suddenly felt as though struck by lightning. On impulse, she rose from her chair, picked up the phone in the kitchen and speed dialed her office. The receptionist answered. "Hey, Susie, this is Pat. I won't be in today. In fact, can you tell the boss I'm really not feeling well and am thinking of taking some time off. I'll let you all know when I can come back."

She hung up, not giving the time for Susie to start asking questions as she knew that whatever she answered would quickly make the rounds of the office. Most of her current cases could be handled by junior staff or interns so she felt no guilt. She did a repeat call to the Guardian's office. She knew how difficult it was to find attorneys who were willing to work pro bono for kids who sometimes may not deserve it, so her temporary disappearance would go unpunished, if not unnoticed. There again, interns could handle whatever cases she was working on.

Her home was free and clear and the income from Bill's estate kept her, what some would say, independently comfortable. She had never taken advantage of this, but now was the time. She climbed the stairs and stopped on the landing. On her right, what had been the master bedroom was now a guest room which had seen very little use over the last few years. It also served as an office, so she walked in, sat at the computer and composed emails to confirm her absence and write brief updates on her cases.

Patricia then moved to the closet where she stored books, old papers and the item she needed now, a suitcase. She then crossed to her own bedroom, the one she used to share with her sister many years ago. It was now decorated in a no nonsense manner. No more frilly vanity or curtains. One double bed, one night table, she knew there would never be a need for two, a triple dresser and a chair.

The closet, almost ten years free of the leaky roof was now larger and well organized. A simple straw carpet covered the refinished wood floor and Venetian blinds blocked the white glare of the morning sun reflecting on the snow.

Patricia walked in, luggage in hand and started packing. She stopped, lifted her head to the ceiling and sighed, remembering a similar event, years ago, but for very different reasons. She shrugged the nostalgic thoughts away and, after basic clothes were packed, wondered what else she should bring. This brought up another question of where she would go.

She was not normally a spontaneous woman and was surprised by the very movements of her hands, sorting clothes out and appearing determined to complete this packing task. She opted to leave things at basics, plus two pairs of pants and a couple of light weight shirts. "If I need anything else, I'll just buy it."

Patricia was glad to hear the snow plow clearing the county road. She had forgotten about the snow hence never considering the fact that she may be snowbound. Now, all she had to do was ram the car through the few inches of snow from her driveway to the road and she was free. She assumed the highways would be cleared already.

Patricia carried her bag to the front door then walked around the house, making sure the windows were locked and adjusting timers for lights to go on and off throughout the evening. She also disconnected the hot water as well as all the small electrical appliances. No sense wasting energy while she was away.

Although she had made no conscious decision as to her destination yet, her car moved from her driveway, headed for the interstate and, with a mind of its own, accessed the southbound lane.

Patricia reflected that the last time she had impulsively started on a long drive, it had begun with the sun behind her and ended hours later, facing its blinding light as she neared her destination. This was going to be different. She was driving into the mid day sun.

A moment of clarity made her question her determination. She considered leaving the highway at the next exit and turning back. But the woman silenced the rational voices in her head and stayed the course.

The snow was gradually melting along the highway. By the time she crossed the state line, there were only puddles reminding her that this year's snow days were over. At least for her.

She stopped at a diner for a late breakfast and filled up the gas tank at the adjacent station. Still unsure as to her ultimate destination, she rolled back onto the highway, confident her reliable wheels would take her somewhere interesting. By the time gas was getting low again, the winter sun had set somewhere to her right and she was getting weary, hundreds of miles of wear and tear on her body.

The Snowbelt and mountains now behind, she didn't worry about the menacing clouds building on the horizon. She was, however tired and stopped at the first decent looking hotel off the highway.

Waking up in a strange bed was something new: Patricia had not left her home since moving back to the farm ten years ago. Disoriented at first, she got her bearings, showered and was on the road again, after grabbing a coffee and donut from the 'breakfast included' table off the hotel lobby.

She knew she should think about where she was going, but wasn't ready for it yet. "Let the car decide", she thought as she padded the dashboard. Filled with gas and determination, the old Volvo decided to continue its southern trek, swerving east when the opportunity came, then onward south again.

Last night's clouds had dispersed and Patricia was occasionally blinded by the sun in spite of her dark glasses. By noon, she had reached a point where heat was winning over cold so she turned the air conditioner on, mentally making a note to stop by some mall along the way for a lighter wardrobe.

By the time she decided to call it a day, she had crossed the Florida state line and was moving along with the traffic on the I- 95, always crowded in spite of the fact that snowbirds were more likely to go home then aim south at this time of year. She decided to drive past Jacksonville and take the St. Augustine exit where an outlet mall, or two as she found out later, was spreading out along the highway.

She registered at a nearby hotel and set out to shop. She had never been a good shopper. She and Bill bought quality clothes so they could wear them for years. Even the Volvo had been purchased with this principle in mind over 12 years ago. Patricia walked into the first store that catered to women, picked a few light pants, capris and tops to try on, discovered she was two sizes larger than she thought and started the process all over again.

She hadn't noticed the weight which had accumulated on her thighs and waist over the years. Seemed like her clothes must have just grown with her, she thought with a smile. She didn't care about the extra pounds; she just wanted to get this painful shopping ordeal over with. Finally, armed with enough to wear for at least a week, and to the delight of the salesclerk, she left and returned to the hotel, making sure she stopped by a fast food restaurant to pick up dinner.

Now, settled on a most uncomfortable upholstered chair with her feet on the bed, she turned the television on and made dinner last as long as she could. Images flashed before her eyes: an episode from Law and Order she remembered watching with Bill. Patricia was transported in time. She had not had one of those time travel experience in a long time. Her heart broke all over again and she switched the station to a lighter fare of sitcom followed by some inane talk show.

Patricia was striving to keep her mind in first gear: she wanted to only function and stay alive, shutting out any thoughts or ideas that may have caused her to dwell on work, home or her late husband. She hence still didn't know where she was headed. That next morning did not bring any insights or inspiration; so she kept going.

Another gas fill-up and hours later, highway signs started posting cities with exotic names like Fort Lauderdale, West Palm Beach, and Miami. Patricia had only seen movies or television shows about those places and was intrigued. Bill had been a fan of Miami Vice years ago. She decided this was a sign and took the first exit towards the beach.

She stopped at the first eye-catching hotel on the beach, hoping she wouldn't have to drive any further, horrified by the traffic which was not of the kind she was accustomed to. She parked near the entrance, admiring the garden paths and serene palm trees swaying in the warm breeze as she was entering the lobby. To her delight, there were vacancies but in spite of her being financially comfortable, with no heirs to inherit later, Patricia was still thrifty. Standing at the reception desk, she negotiated a deal for a week stay, insisting on a room with ocean view and a balcony.

In her room, Patricia stepped outside the patio door and faced the Atlantic. She felt as if a load was sliding off her shoulders like a waterfall washes down the dead leaves of fall. She smiled and consciously let that feeling of quietude replace the stress which had been accumulating over the last few years. She allowed one layer of thoughts to come back and sorted out memories of all the good times she had lived through in the six decades of her life.

This was the same peace she had known while married to Bill: a tranquil state of mind, rarely, if ever disturbed by fights or arguments between two people who had truly been made for each other. She never thought she could achieve this mental state alone.

Patricia made herself comfortable on a white lounge chair and allowed her body to relax and share her mind's comfort. Looking at the view, she wondered why she and Bill never traveled and smiled remembering her husband's aversion to change. She had not missed it then, but pondered about perhaps turning a new leaf in her life's history. "Tomorrow will take care of itself" she thought. "Today is the first day of the rest of my life" she closed her eyes and smiled at her own pathetic clichés. Her face caressed by a soft sea breeze and her whole being soothed by the sounds of sea and birds, she fell into a dreamless sleep.

The days were drifting by, one moment following another; Patricia was at peace. One evening, as she was enjoying dinner at the hotel and watching cruise ships approach the port, a couple walked by and the man pointed out to sea. "This is the one we'll be on, I think." He said. His wife grabbed his arm and excitedly nodded. "I can't wait. A whole week of nowhere to go and nothing to do."

This caught Patricia's fancy. She tried to see which ship the man was pointing at, but they all looked the same to her. She finished her meal and walked over to the concierge desk where brochures boasting about everything from day trips to shopping excursions, night clubbing and tourists attractions were displayed for the benefit of the guests.

One pamphlet caught Patricia's attention. A large vessel was depicted in some southern paradise with beaches and mountains on the horizon. She picked that one as well as others with similar appeal and went to her room to study the information. She first lined up her collection on the bed then, after eliminating cruises that appear to be either too long or too expensive, she ended up with two to choose from. Both were leaving just as her hotel reservation ran out, both were aiming south, one to Costa Rica and the other to the Bahamas and some other place she had never heard of. Everybody goes to Costa Rica, she thought, discarding the flyer, which left only one option.

Before she knew it, she was on the phone with a cruise line agent, making reservations to leave as soon as the week was up. There were no cabins with balconies available, but, it was a ship, there were bound to be many outdoor areas from which to see the sights and relax. The way things were going, she wondered if she'd be back home in time to pay for all these credit card expenses; however, this seemed unimportant at this time.

On the day she was to leave, Patricia checked one more time on her Volvo which was staying in the safety of the hotel parking lot. She then gave the desk clerk a key, in case of emergency, and took a taxi to the port where she was to board her new home for the next week.

Apart from hotel employees and the cruise line agent, she had not had a single conversation with another human being since her brief telephone conversation with the law firm and the Guardian's receptionists. And that was fine with this woman who had never been much of a conversationalist.

The first night on board, she was seated in the dining room with a couple traveling with their three teenagers. The 18 year old was going to leave for college after graduating in June and the family had decided that this vacation may be their last with the entire clan. The 14 and 16 year olds were pleasant enough but the older boy talked nothing but football and kept asking if they would be back in time to see the current reality show he was addicted to. He also periodically moaned about the favorite sports events he would be missing.

In light of the conversation, most of which was hijacked by the whiny, obnoxious boy, Patricia remained quiet during the meal, occasionally nodding if her approval was required, but not joining in any particular discourse. She made a mental note to avoid the dining room and eat at one of the many buffet tables set up throughout the ship or to request another table.

Her days were spent on a lawn chair as far from the pool as she could manage, trying to avoid the giddy crowd which tended to accumulate there from morning to dusk and the drunks crowding the hot tub. She could have chosen another location, but, the front of the ship was too windy, the back was occupied by a teen activity center and, in reality, she didn't mind the din of people having a good time. It was a nice change from what she was used to in the court room. Her nights were mostly consisting of dinner and a book. One evening she followed some fellow cruisers into a club and admittedly enjoyed the live entertainment, the drinks with paper umbrellas attached to tropical fruits and came close to mingling with some passengers.

Another night, she took in a movie after spending the day in some busy island port, walking around like a zombie, finding no interest in the local colors. "Something must be wrong with me." She wondered.

Everyone else seemed so taken by the obvious tourist traps, but she just didn't find any appeal in the overcrowded markets filled with so-called local artifacts. She could tell that there was nothing local about the various trinkets. Most were made in Taiwan or China. She also thought it obvious that what looked like individually owned boutiques were, in fact, one supermarket sized area, likely owned by one exploitive owner who hired local families to sell.

Other buildings were colorful but needing of paint. The local residents looked happy but their smiles often turned into frowns once the tourists were out of sight. She overheard a shopkeeper complaining about these 'boat people' who eat and drink on the ship and always haggle on prices so the locals, hired to sell the souvenirs, made no money.

Patricia decided to walk farther into the heart of the town where she found genuine native art, buying a few trinkets for people back at her office. She saw business men and women entering office buildings and felt more comfortable there. The tourist area with its bars filled with drunken cruisers, the shops with fake native wares didn't hold any interest for her. After three hours of walking aimlessly, she decided to cut the shore leave short and perhaps enjoy the quieter atmosphere of the ship since most of her fellow passengers were on shore.

She now had at least three layers of brain working and a fourth one was crawling in. From her functioning phase, to her directional level, she was now in her learning mode and fast accessing her judgmental and decision making areas.

The last stop was in a place which she had never heard of. She had resolved to stay aboard so she could enjoy some of the water activities abandoned by the crowds for the local beaches. She ate a drawn out breakfast and went for a stroll on deck to see what this last so-called paradise was like.

As she reached the point where a large expanse of beach was visible, she knew this place was different. She stood motionless for what may have been two hours before the ship anchored near the local port. This one was nothing like the other island. She was breathless. Visitors had to board a smaller craft to go on shore since the narrow cove was too shallow to accommodate the cruise ship. Leaning on the railing, she stared at the town with its adobe homes, all prim and proper. She watched the small fishing boats which surrounded her monstrous floating palace and liked the faces of the men and women calmly handling the task of finding food for their families or to sell at the market. They were all impervious to the tourists landing on their beaches and this, in itself, made the island that much more attractive to Patricia.

"Isn't this wonderful." Someone muttered next to her. She turned to notice the captain, whom she recognized from the night he had held a welcoming reception in the theatre. Patricia nodded. "Yes." Is all she could say. "Makes you want to drop everything and stay, doesn't it?" the man asked. She nodded again. "Yes."

Then it happened: his last statement had caused her last layer of brain to go into high gear. Patricia turned to the Captain. "Is there a way one can leave this boat and maybe catch another later?" He turned, surprised. "I don't think there is a company policy about abandoning ship." He said in a teasing manner, correcting her reference to his vessel as a boat rather than a ship.

Then he got serious and stopped to think. "However, if you wanted to do something like this, nothing keeps you from flying back or seeing if there is room in the next voyage." He hesitated. He could not figure out if this quiet, ordinary-looking woman was really asking for information, or whether she was just wishful thinking and musing out loud. "I also think that if you came back on a later cruise, the cruise line may charge for another passage. Also the local authorities may frown on this." He thought further. "I don't think anyone has ever done this since I've been working for the cruise line. The only thing I would say is that you would have to tell us so we don't attempt to find you

when you fail to board the ship before we sail at dusk."
He smiled.

This was more than Patricia wanted to know.
She had never felt such an impulse before. She had to
go ashore, be on this island, at least for a while.
Something was pulling her there. "All right," she said,
digging into her bag, "here is my business card with my
name and information, consider me AWOL." She
laughed at her own words and before the captain had a
chance to react, ran up to her cabin to pack.

An hour later and out of breath, Patricia was on
the quay, wondering what got into her that caused such
a rash decision. She came close to panic, but reasoned
that what was done was done and she may as well
continue on this path to see where it led. She was
searched by a customs agent, surprised by a woman
carrying a suitcase for what was to be a few hours. But
she offered her business card and went into a long
tirade about staying on for a week or so. Perhaps
because the agent's English did not include a stark
raving man women talking at the speed of light, all
went well. Authorities on this island did not appear
quite as obsessed with rules as they are in major ports
so he waved her on and Patricia walked into town.

She stopped to buy postcards and watched other
tourists earnestly shopping. She also bought and
changed into loud colored shorts and shirt, something

she hadn't worn, probably ever. Patricia's body was not shorts-friendly, but she no longer cared. Her white legs could have been compared to those of a pale chicken with formidable appendages, and the over sized arms protruding from the sleeves were wanting of a sun kiss. Suitcase in hand, looking like a large duck, she noticed a group of kids staring at her, smiled at them and laughed at her own reflection in a store window.

After a glorious lunch of scallops and greens, garnished with fresh fruits, she started inquiring about lodging. As much as the island was beautiful, sleeping on the beach was out of the question. When she heard the name "My Last Dream" her choice was made. She only hoped they had a room. Her Spanish was quite rudimentary so she was afraid of calling. She decided to just show up.

A taxi dropped her off in front of the quaint hotel, which looked like a large private villa, and she walked into the lobby, no more spacious than an average living room. Once inside, however, she saw that the room opened up to an enormous solarium where tables were set up. Beyond that, one could see the terrace, landscaped around a pool and then the ocean, framed by palm trees and rows of flowering shrubs.

She was surprised, but happily so, that they had a room available. It didn't have an ocean view, but, being on the first floor, the room had its own private terrace which would allow her to come and go as she pleased. A middle aged woman, her blond hair bound in a pony tail and wearing a tasteful Bermuda shorts outfit came to welcome her. She was glad everyone spoke English but didn't have a need for conversation and quickly left to unpack, wondering about this party the woman had invited her to attend tomorrow night. As soon as she had unpacked her bags, she fell on the bed, mentally and physically exhausted. What on earth had she done? Then she remembered Miss Volvo, all by herself, still parked somewhere in Miami, smiled and allowed her mind to roam into a different space and time just before she fell asleep.

##

CROSSING THE DREAM LINE

Part II

My Last Dream

JULIE

Monday. I have no clue what date it is, but I'm quite sure it's Monday. I haven't written a word in over ten years, apart, of course, from financial reports or articles for the Journal, all of which are now things of the past. It's been a rough ride, but, considering where I am now, I'd say it was worth the pain. I found my old diary when I went back at Christmas. So I decided to bring here if only to keep anyone from reading it, but now that I have lots of time on my hands, why not pick up where I left off?

Ah. I can hear the surf gently caressing the beach and guess at the tiny bubbles of what looks like soap, but can't possibly be, forming along the beach line. Oops, the sun just reached the tip of my toes which are no longer safe under the umbrella. This is MY terrace. This is MY beach, MY sun. Beats a decrepit cabin on some godforsaken mountain with drunken hunters lurking around, I would say. This slice of my life from the past feels so unreal. It's like it never happened. I'm really glad I wrote about it at the time, otherwise I would be sure I dreamed it up. I can now write, in retrospect: Was I out of my mind? Turning fifty was nothing. And I had all these friends around me. My family seemed to tolerate me. What the hell was I thinking?

Was my little half-century jaunt, running away from home, so to speak, and ending up in a mountain cabin ... ok, the nature part was cool, but the hunters' scare and freezing my ass off... worth it? I guess so. I learned a lot about myself then: baby, you may be clever, but you're no rough-in gal. I also gained a lot of perspective on my life.

I'm expecting Josée, Jon and the kids later this week. I'm not sure how I feel about that. I've had 'issues' with my eldest child lately but she may overlook them seeing that this is the ideal time to escape the damp cold of early spring in the city and enjoy a summer-like respite. Besides, I really think they owe me a visit. Love the grandkids, though the boys are a little 'busy' to put it mildly and Josée sort of ignores them while Jon encourages their questionable behavior. That said, they can be adorable and I can't wait to get a few hugs, provided they haven't grown out of them yet, considering I haven't seen them in months. Richard, now a long-distance mate, promised to fly over with them as well and drag Jake if he can get him away from his books.

Ah, better put the pen away. Here comes my pride and joy. Maybe I'll ask him to bring his brood over for dinner. He never gets around to organizing his life in spite of his wife's attempt at domesticating him. Well, I look at it that way, it's better he is settled here with a family and sort of a job, then chasing god knows what pot of gold at the end of an elusive rainbow as he did back home.

Back home. I'll have to pick up on that later. What is 'back home' now? The Westchester County dream estate on the golf course? My little corner of paradise right here? I'm not sure where home is anymore.

11 AM yes, they're all coming for dinner. I love it. We usually eat here on the patio then the kids play in the sand or take a nap in the hammock. That's what life is about.

Anyway, back to home or whatever. I haven't been there since the holidays and only remember my visit as an insane round of parties, trips to the mall to buy presents no one will use or wear, too much drinking and an extra ten pounds of fat added to the mix. I couldn't wait to come back to what is, I have now rationalized, home to me. It's hard to imagine that this rat race was my life for so many years.

Lately I've begun to think about people I have known for years in different ways. Maybe because once I removed myself from their circle, they started inventing stories about our relationships and now they treat me as if I were a stranger. I guess a psychologist would probably say it's some sort of separation anxiety thing: if you convince yourself that the person who left is unworthy, it is much easier to let her go. I just don't feel comfortable in my own skin when I'm in social situations with people I thought were trusty old friends. I feel as though I've never known anyone, really, and they definitely have no clue of who I am now. What frightens me the most is that I don't seem to have figured out who I am either. I guess you could call it some sort of identity crisis. Hmm.

##

The guests are slowly crawling on to the terrace surrounding the pool, tanned, relaxed and holding various drink concoctions dreamed up by Ricardo, my adorable bar tender. Funny most look to be about my age. I suppose this place is in one of the still affordable beach destinations and since this is a repurposed former estate, there are fewer rooms hence less other tourists to be a hassle. I don't know about anyone else, but as I get older, I'm not so much into the chichi expensive resorts where all that counts is that you spend as much money as possible, and where the staff is only polite to get better tips. I've been on that road before, now I want people to like me for myself, not my money. My hotel accommodates that wish. It's almost like a bed and breakfast, except for the pool bar and the occasional lunch barbeque. I also pay my staff well enough that they are happy and treat all the guests as special regardless of their financial status.

Here's Lucy. There's an unusual woman. I think she may be a bit older. She always appears as if she's looking for something or someone. It's hard to describe. She doesn't strike me as an adventurous type, she always picks the same spot on the beach... but, I don't know, she is here on her own, after all. Her baggy turquoise shorts and Hawaiian shirt don't help the sort of middle class frumpy look she carries everywhere with her. Maybe I'll start a conversation. Naw, not now. But, I am curious to know what brought her here in this little known island resort.

Idea: Maybe I should start googling my guests before they come, pretend I'm psychic and tell their fortune. Hmm, I don't think that would be very ethical... fun though.

##

LUCY

Lucy was walking through the solarium, then on to the beach when she saw other guests enjoying tropical drinks. Why not? She thought. Now, standing near the pool, Pina Colada in hand, she isn't sure if she should try to start a conversation with someone or just sit at one of the tables and enjoy the mellow mood the drink is bringing on.

She knows Jackie won't be here for a few days but really looks forward to her arrival. When Jackie had first told her about coming along to this resort, she wasn't sure it was such a good idea. She didn't know her that well and had plans to write during most of her stay. As it turns out, she now feels like a month is long time to spend on a beach with nothing to do, especially since she hasn't been able to concentrate enough to even start writing. This is a wonderful resort, the people are friendly, the owner, the little she has seen of her, also looks nice, but she wonders how long she can stay here and not get bored to tears.

Lucy isn't the type to explore on her own and so far, no one has made a move to indicate that her company would be welcome. After the first few days of enjoying the beach and walking around town, she was at a loss for activities. She bought a few used books in an antique shop and has already read two of them. She'll have to go back for more if she is to survive a month here. Although, she reflects, life may get a bit more interesting once Jackie gets here.

She finishes her drink, and, with a curious glance through the bushes towards the owner's villa, she continues on to the beach to pick up a bite to eat from one of the food huts, and then spend the rest of the afternoon reading.

The beach is quiet, unlike last weekend when local kids organized volleyball games, Frisbee competitions and other activities. These antics had caused white sand to splatter and mess up Lucy's comfortable station, but also to create an air of festive energy which she enjoyed.

She dreads dinner. She thinks it is one thing to eat alone at home, but yet another to go out and face couples and families dining together while you just sit on your own and stare. After the first night, she took to getting take-out from the huts on the beach and eating at a table by the swimming pool. It will be a long month the way things are going.

She lifts her head from the book and stares at the ocean. Apart from seeing the expanse of water from her flight to Africa, she has never been on a tropical beach before. Her first timid steps in the amazing turquoise water were like receiving a sacrament. She, who has never learned to swim, could almost feel herself floating in the warm salty water. This alone, she thinks, makes the trip worthwhile. She knows that after her body sheds every trace of stress and worry, she will surely find something to do with her time, but for the time being, she just lets life happen around her and reads.

##

JULIE

Tuesday. Josée called. They're not coming. Some sort of kids' issue. Didn't sound very convincing. I'm happy I didn't let myself get too excited about their visit. I'll tell the manager to open up the rooms. Richard is still on for now, but who knows.

My sweet Christopher and his family did come over for dinner last night and I'm glad they did. Who would have thought that the one child I had virtually given up on is the one who is so important to me now? When I moved here, he only came down here with me just for 'something goofy to do', but instantly fell in love with the beach, the island lifestyle and… Theresa.

Theresa is the most precious, petite woman, with long black hair and piercing brown eyes I have ever met. Under this angelic appearance, however, lies a will of steel which, as it turns out, is what Christopher needed all along.

We met her while taking a walk on the beach. She was selling local artifacts, some which she had created herself, others crafted by home bound women or artists too old to peddle their own wares. Under the guise of learning Spanish, Christopher enrolled her help and, before the year was out, he was married with Daniela on the way, soon to be followed by Roberto, Toto to most of us. Island babies live mostly naked all day and radiate a sense of freedom I have never seen before. Every time I set eyes on my grandchildren, I feel so much love and peace that the guilt in having abandoned my country, family and friends is forgotten for a while. They are a little confused between their mother's Spanish, Christopher's Spanglish and my English, but we are all learning together and they are being oh so cute about it.

A few months ago, Christopher built a shop with his own hands on a small piece of land near the main tourist area. (I would never have believed he could do that in a thousand years!) He now hustles tourists and sells an array of artistic creations and some questionable native crafts. I have never seen him so happy. This definitely adds to my wondering if we ever really know anyone, even when we carried him for nine months and raised him to manhood.

If I had to guess, I would have thought he would end up in the music business, if only as a flunky... something like a 'dead head' of the 80's. Life works in strange and mysterious ways! My middle son, the island entrepreneur, married with two children. After that, nothing can surprise me.

Back to moi. Three years ago, I finally got tired of favoritism, sexism and office politics. I got into this huge argument with the managing partner and stormed out of his office. My last words, which I knew I may regret, but loved saying, were "I quit." To be fair, I thought resigning would mean former colleagues seeking me out for advice, faithful clients for whom I had made millions hiring me to consult on their portfolio and I was sort of excited at the prospect. I sent some feelers, but what I found was that once removed from the playing field, I became a non-entity, as though I never existed or spent almost 30 years catering to everyone. (No one knows this, but I actually tried to get my job back, only to face something akin to 'I told you so', from my former partners, in addition to the tirade about economic downturn, leaving room for the younger brokers (read lower compensation) etc...) A humiliating experience I wouldn't wish on anyone.

After brooding for a while, I immersed myself in the country club life which proved to be a lot more work than play. Richard loved having me at home and was relying on me for, well, everything. Between organizing parties and tournaments, being on various boards and committees, house management work... well, that definitely was not for me.

So one night, after watching an episode of my favorite international real estate show, I went to my computer and started surfing for island property (pun intended). I was just playing at it, a way to take my mind off reality, but then I came across this adorable hotel and the wheels were in motion. Under the pretense of a vacation, I arranged for Richard and me to visit the island and the inn. I fell in love instantly.

When we went back, I cashed-in my personal portfolio and whatever savings I had, flew back down here and bought this place. Ten guestrooms, a small breakfast area, wrap around decks that lead to a terrace and pool-side bar then the beach, not to mention my own tiny villa with all windows facing the ocean and bright red flowering shrubs strategically placed for privacy. I can see my guests around the pool and check on the bartender but while it is possible for someone to spy on me through the thicket, it requires more effort. I spent the first year getting my bearings and organizing the business, and then it took me almost as long to decompress and engage my brain into island gear. By that time I was a grandmother and basked into that glorious state for a while. Lately, however, I've been finding myself more interested in the guests.

Well, all and all, I live in paradise without being a burden to anyone. Hey, I'm actually starting to make money on the joint, a good thing since I no longer have retirement funds or savings cushion whatsoever! I can just hear my sister telling everyone how whatever I touch turns to gold. I hope she's right... and, sorry, I can't help it.

This is it in a nutshell. I can't say Richard was thrilled, but by then I was at what I thought was the end of the line, so his opinion mattered less than it should have. In any case, we're having this awesome long distance relationship which seems to be working well for both of us. It's his decision anyway: in his technological field, armed with computers and other electronic paraphernalia, he could work anywhere if he wanted to. He just chooses not to and I respect him for it. He'll be here when he's ready. Besides, Jake still needs him. I guess I'm just a selfish bitch. I'm allowed. I'm sixty and I can tell everyone to fuck themselves if I want to. I wonder if they put people away here when they start laughing out loud when no one is around. Something to ponder...

Jake is almost 16 now and, as I always thought he would, attending a prestigious prep school, excelling at everything he starts, focusing on the positive and astounding his professors and peers with his academic accomplishments. He grew up to be quite good looking, a younger version of his dad, but he's not as easy to get close to, always in a world of his own. We never connected very well. He was so grown-up like, even as a child. He never really played with toys except an erector set, and some convolutedly transformable super heroes.

To be honest, I think I sometimes felt intimidated by the way he seemed to always know what I was thinking. I know he judged me, I saw it when I got back from my fateful mountain escape and more so when I resigned from my job and gave up all that money. He still doesn't understand why I did that. I worry that he has no girlfriend yet and voices no interests in activities teenagers should be attracted to. He only learned to drive because he chooses to still live at home and commute to school. Richard says he's just a late bloomer. I hope so. I miss him. In fact, I miss them all. But that sun feels damned good. Besides, he's coming to work at the hotel this summer, so we'll have plenty of time to catch up.

Oh, here comes the 'Mr. and Mrs.' I caught that nickname from the staff: these two are inseparable. They rise together, they go to the beach in unison, eat the same things... Makes you wonder if they do synchronized swimming. I don't think anyone has ever seen them apart. Personally, I think she looks more like a puppy dog than a loving wife and he strikes me as a bit of an ass... but then that's just me being unduly critical.

I guess they are probably the epitome of middle class marriages that last forever: no sparks, no fun, but damn if they don't stay together for the duration. Barbara and Grant forever. Nice, maybe, but definitely not for me.

##

BARBARA

Barbara and Grant walked toward the beach where they moved two hotel lounge chairs closer to the water, just at the level where the surf collapses on the shore. They were now parked on the wet sand, feeling a salty lick of water on their backs as each wave reached the beach.

The couple had arrived a few days before and toured the island, first with a guide, then on their own. Barbara had never seen anything like it. The sky seemed bluer, the mountains had cleaner edges, even the salt water felt softer. She had been to different beaches many times as a child, first with her parents, then at summer camp, but the east coast American waters, even the gulf coast beaches, looked nothing like this.

She noticed Grant getting a little restless and encouraged him to go for a swim. He shook his head and closed his eyes. She watched him as he finally fell asleep on the chair. Barbara was now free to take her book out and enjoy her favorite way to pass the time. She was so concentrated on her reading that she failed to notice the tide rising. It wasn't until some water reached up and almost snatched the book out of her hand that she realized time had just flown by and the sun was getting closer to the horizon.

She woke Grant and together they brought the chairs back up the beach and walked up to their room to change for dinner.

The staff was perfectly polite, but Barbara felt that some gave them peculiar looks, something which made her feel self-conscious, but after a couple of days, she failed to notice them anymore. In fact although she would have liked to meet new people, she now avoided all contact with both the employees of the hotel and other guests. She knew Grant wasn't much into socializing and, although he had deemed this vacation as her birthday present, it was still his vacation.

They showered, dressed and set out to find dinner. The night was mild and scented with flowers that only bloom after sundown. Even Grant looked more relaxed and seemed to enjoy the walk to town. Barbara took his arm and savored the moment.

##

JULIE

Wednesday. When I bought this hotel, I made sure it was a 'turnkey' proposition, one that included both furniture and staff. However, somehow it seems to always require work on my part. I just spent the morning convincing a guest that her room was not haunted. The noises came from the sea breeze oozing around the old hurricane shutters. And, I swear this is one of the sanest complaints I've had in the short time since I've been here. I'm learning.

I can't believe I'm sixty now (am I dwelling on this?). Seems like fifty was such a young age and I wonder why I made such a big deal of it at the time. Sixty, now that's a landmark!

Oops, my brain is starting to drop into a negative cycle… I no longer allow it to do so I will therefore go for a long walk on the beach and a well deserved swim.

I see Betsy is going for a swim as well. She's only been here a couple of days and has the staff fawning all over her. Although her accent is quite different from that of the local population, her Spanish is flawless. She is always so grateful for whatever anyone does for her.

Not so long ago, I may have thought of her as a pathetic do-gooder, but, I don't know, she looks so much happier than most of us here, really. With the loose cotton wrap that shows her old fashioned bathing suit and her long gray hair held up by a silver barrette she looks like a paradox in time and age.

She puzzles me. She has class but not in the way a country club member would interpret it. She just radiates class and serenity. I should make an effort to talk to her. Maybe I'll run into her on the beach... maybe tomorrow.

##

BETSY

Betsy sits on a lounge chair away from other bathers, takes a pen and paper out of her bag and starts to write.

"Dear Father Pascal," she puts her pen down. What can she say? She has been here only a few days and is already making friends with the entire population. She can't believe this is happening to her. She can enjoy the culture she loves, but without the dramas usually associated with guests of La Casa. She thinks that if the children seeking refuge in her home saw how others like them can be so happy, they probably would stand a better chance of success as they grew up. As it is, those poor city kids look around them and often only see hopelessness and poverty.

It makes her wonder if this is how prejudices against certain races or religions are born. If those who are poor, look different or pray to a different god are not what we refer to as 'winners', then they become 'losers' in other words, people of lesser value.

Betsy's thoughts are getting confused. She is a loser in every sense of the way: she is poor, she is a housekeeper for a mission, plus, she is old and has no bright or any other kind of future prospects. But then again, why is she so happy? She shakes her head to chase those thoughts away and continues writing her letter.

"I am so grateful to everyone for this vacation. I'm learning new Spanish expressions and the accent here is adorable. I just love the people of the island. Even the staff is being super nice to me. How are you?"

Betsy rereads the bit she wrote, sighs and puts the pen and paper back in her beach bag. She has never been one to write letters and this is just typical of how she can't relay interesting information on paper. She envies people who just pick up a pen and make magic with the words.

She starts thinking about her experience with the ocean when she first arrived in New York. She had taken a subway to Coney Island and watched the kids playing on the beach. That was the only beach she had ever seen in person.

Over the last ten years, the Midwestern woman has never felt the need to visit the Jersey shore or Long Island. She wonders if those beaches are like the ones here, but is afraid to ask. She hears the hotel owner is from New York as well and hopes she can talk about this with her without looking too naïve or silly. She finally decides that this being a tropical beach, it has to be unique. Bored by her own train of thoughts, she closes the door to it by making a mental note to agree the next time one of the girls or someone from La Casa asks her to accompany them to the shore.

##

JULIE

Thursday. Richard isn't coming either, work issues, which means Jake is out. Bummer.

It's 3:30 (pm) and I wonder what I'll do tonight. I usually read, visit with friends or enjoy my son's family, but I sometimes just stare at the ocean and watch the moon rise with my favorite wine. That sounds good. I think maybe I'll organize a party for Saturday night. I'll ask Theresa if she knows of any good guitar player to entertain us… hmm that should be fun and… get my mind off the missing family links.

8 PM. Didn't get much done today. It took a couple of years, but the island lifestyle is rubbing off on me. Went to the market, walked around for a while, stopped by to see Daniela and Toto, got my daily dose of hugs and came home. I ran into Betsy on the way back and we chatted for a bit. She's an intriguing woman. I couldn't get much out of her except that she has two daughters and a grandson in New York, all of whom she obviously dotes on. We then talked about the city and how much she enjoyed it and I missed it. That's it. Yes, I think a party, with lots of drinking to loosen up everyone's proper manners and we can all have fun. I'll make a list of things we need.

10 PM. The moon is awesome tonight. It's shining through one of the palm trees on the beach and

leaves a trail of light on the sand. I hear the surf and can only smile. Too bad the family is missing out on such serenity. It makes you question your entire crazy life of running from one busy activity to the next without pause.

God, my mind wonders. I can't seem to focus on any one subject. The wine? Hmm, maybe. For some reason, a shadow has just crossed my mind and a recurring sadness rises in my throat. How dramatic. Well, maybe I should write about it and get it over with; otherwise, I may never get past it. Here goes. My sixtieth birthday. Oh God.

That fateful day was a few months ago. Richard was coming over. I was getting excited. After the party in my honor ten years ago, I figured there would be a plane load of friends, family and hangers-on to help me forget the very notion of being sixty.

My birthday isn't in the best vacation season, but still, it's summer all year long here, so we can make it the best vacation season! A free room at the inn was also an incentive. Besides, everyone I know can afford it. I didn't book any rooms that week and made many hints to that effect with the kids and whoever called. (My first mistake.) I knew I could be disappointed, but I kept thinking about the kids, and everyone I had left behind and how much I missed them. I also told Richard many times that all the rooms were free and all

I really wanted was to be with my family. He didn't seem to care, but that would be just like him to sound aloof. I didn't make any plans, not even with Christopher. Better to let everything be, so good things can happen.

In retrospect, this was a very stupid and selfish thing to do, expecting others not only to cater to me because I was turning sixty, but to also guess what I wanted. But, sorry that's just the way it was.

OK. I know I promised myself I wasn't going to be negative, but that was before I had my third glass of wine. Now I say, let's just do it. I deserve a good negative once in a while. Heck, maybe I'll even cry. What the hell. Let's be wild.

Anyway, I picked up Richard at the airport. He was glad to be here, well… anyone who flies lately is glad to get anywhere… but I digress. We retrieved his luggage and drove home. Did I say I have the cutest little electric car? Anyway, this was on my birthday eve. I'd asked him to bring a few of my favorite treats from home but he forgot. Well, no big deal. There's tomorrow. I checked my cupboard to see if we would have enough champagne glasses for at least the immediate family and found I may have to borrow some from the bar. But that's OK. It's my hotel, right?

I thought maybe we'd go out to eat that night, but Richard was tired from the trip and said he preferred eating at home. We defrosted steaks threw them on the barbeque with potatoes and a pile of fresh vegetables. The wine flowed and I was giving in to feeling good about what was coming next.

I was up early, ready for phone calls or visitors or just ready. We had breakfast at the hotel, the dining room was strangely silent on such a gorgeous day. We took our shoes off and headed for the beach.. As we were walking in silence, Richard reached into his pocket and a nicely wrapped box appeared. He stopped, gave me a hug and handed me my birthday present. The 'forever' diamond necklace was exquisite. Something I would probably be terrified to wear for fear of losing it, but it was incredibly sweet of him to offer this token of what may look broken to others, but was still forever as far as we were concerned.

By the time we walked back, I had a happy birthday message from an old (literally) friend from college. Nothing else. Well, I thought, planes haven't landed yet. Looking back on it, Richard should have nipped my hopes in the bud. He must have known nothing would happen.

My mood started deteriorating as the morning wore off. I was not, by any means angry: how can you be angry when you find no one bothers to come or, so far, call? It's not their fault that you abandoned them. You finally realize how you are just not a nice person. All what you believed was right about yourself turns around in your head until you see yourself as a dark version of the person you thought you were, if that makes any sense. I had to conclude that given the same circumstances, I probably would have boycotted my birthday as well.

A messenger dropped by with two boxes. One had flowers from Josée and family. An interesting choice considering I live surrounded by tropical colors but I still loved them; however, this was not a good augur. The second had a professional picture album with shots from when I was born until now and including an accurate, but quite cold micro-biography of my pathetic life. Hear this: Born, graduated, got married, had this baby girl, (the order was a little mixed, but moving on) then a son and traveled a few times, and then the third child, then moved away.

This was Jake being sweet. I had tears in my eyes thinking how hard it must have been to find all these old photos and put them all together. He surprisingly understood that birthdays are supposed to be the one day a year when the person celebrating has a right to be totally selfish. Now all I needed were the people to show up.

We lunched on tostadas and margaritas from a beach hut. Christopher saw us strolling by, waved at his dad 'hey dad, long time no see' and rushed to sweep me off my feet to wish me a happy birthday. "Theresa wants you to come to dinner tonight, OK?" I just let Richard answer. I was touched and thrilled but, I admit, still waiting for something grander to happen. Richard quickly agreed, saying we'd be there early to play with the kids before dinner.

By that time, I knew all the flights connecting to the US had landed and left to return to the mainland. Arriving at the hotel just served as a reminder of what I had done: there was no one there. I made arrangements for the rooms to be back on the market immediately and tried hard to hide my disappointment from Richard, but he knew there was something wrong. We went for a quick swim and had a pomegranate martini on the patio before strolling over to Christopher's house.

Christopher and Theresa radiated with joy. Daniela gave me dozens of drawings, still obscure in subject, but showing definite potential. Toto just smiled and handed me an indefinable finger painted abstract. Theresa was excited to give me a beautiful, brightly colored sundress she had designed and sewed herself.

After a few more drinks, the heartfelt love I sensed from this family had me feeling happy and fulfilled... until the next day when I discovered voice mail messages, one from Josée saying 'by the way, happy birthday, hope you liked the flowers.' The other from Jake, 'Hey, happy birthday mom, hope you got the package.'

Ok, I know it's wrong, I know I should never expect anything, but never in my life have I ever asked anyone for anything. All my women friends who had turned 60 had been the subject of roasts by lesser known comics, like family members, parties with hired bands, one was even flown to Paris so she could celebrate in style with her family.

The one time in my life when it was important to feel loved by everyone again, to feel validated in what perhaps bad decisions I had made, that one time, no one felt the need to give it to me... well, except Christopher, that is. Richard was there, but he knew I wanted my children around me. He should have told them. As it were, he was surprised to see me so upset.

Anyway, writing this makes me feel selfish, and ungrateful, which brings me to the next issue. By that time, I was questioning my own identity and made the biggest mistake of all. I thought that once your children are almost as old as you, you should be able to confide and express emotions which may not be justified but are real nonetheless. I should have counted to a thousand before putting ink to paper.

Actually I didn't think it was that bad. I thank them profusely for the gifts, told about my new necklace from their dad and the awesome dinner with Christopher's family. I just added that I couldn't shake the sadness of not having had my whole family with me on that day.

I thought this would be taken for what it was, a passing but overwhelming feeling of loss and utter disappointment, but it wasn't. Josée took it personally since she knows that while Jake may have had the excuse of school and exams, she, on the other hand was an established dentist with a built-in replacement, often taking time off for traveling with the kids or going to a health spa. Even her husband Jon now owns his own mechanics shop and can get away whenever he wants.

So, I admit I may have overreacted, but I was the one turning 60 and, for once in my life, I think I should have been allowed to feel sorry for myself. Well, that's about it in a nut shell. Life will never be the same again. I sent the same letter to Jake, but he replied that he never knew I would feel this way, apologized and promised to come as soon as he could get away (not now obviously). I think this was a good response. Things are back to normal as far as he is concerned.

Funny how all of this made me question my entire being: have I been fooling myself that I was a generous, loving person all these years? I guess I wasn't. It's so weird to see your life from a different, perhaps even more realistic perspective.

I just re-read some of the entries of my half century escapade and see how Josée could have felt left out of my life. But... she was so self-reliant, almost selfish in her own refusal for help or support: always knowing what she wanted, confident and self-assured, I never even thought she ever needed me but somehow knew I needed her more as my dependable, strong oldest child. Boy, was I wrong!

One lesson I learned that day, is that the saying that goes like 'good things happen to those who wait' makes no sense at all. Good things eventually happen to everyone whether they wait or not. However, bad things happen to those who wait as well, but mostly NOTHING happens to those who wait. Wine really gets the philosopher out of me!

Shit, I had too much to drink. I must have killed the whole bottle while I was writing. Not good. I think I'll go for a walk on the beach to clear my head... it needs it badly!

11:30 PM. When I walked back to my cottage, I saw Clara sitting on the terrace, staring at the water.

153

She arrived from London yesterday and said a friend would join her. Hair cropped close to the scalp, she holds herself straight, even in the lounge chair, and seems like a strong but gentle woman. Her cotton African caftan with its rich tones of red and yellow blends well with the full moon shining on the water and accentuates her own dark skin. She must have been stunning as a young woman. Actually she is still extraordinarily attractive. I wonder what brings her here.

##

CLARA

Clara has only been here a day and already feels the benefit of ocean air and relaxing island mood. She was born on an island. The place where she grew up in Jamaica wasn't anything like this resort, but in some ways this still has the feeling of home. She couldn't get enough of the soft ocean breeze and the smells and sounds of nature's night life.

"I have come full circle." She thinks to herself. "Born on an island, and maybe destined to die on an island." She smiles, thinking ironically that even if she dies in England, it would still be an island.

She has finally reached the stage where she doesn't question her fate. The doctors have rendered their verdict and she is here to say goodbye to the only friend who always stood by her through her tumultuous life. When she received the vacation package, she had no idea what it meant since no one but her kids knew of her short time left, but she was glad. She could never have afforded this on her own and going back to New York for a visit would have been too painful. She shuddered and chased those memories away.

She is excited about seeing her friend one last time, but in the meantime, she sits by the pool or on the beach, only grabbing food from the closest beach hut every so often. She feels no pressure or need for any other distractions or entertainment. Her friend couldn't have picked a better place for a final goodbye.

##

JULIE

Friday. Another beautiful day in paradise as they say at the tourist office. It really is. I talked to the staff and we're set to have an island bash tomorrow night. Should be fun.

It's become such a habit to write in this journal that I can't drink coffee without it anymore. I guess it's like those with cigarette addictions: coffee = cigarette, drink = cigarettes, with me it's coffee = writing. Thank god no one in the family ever got into this nasty smoking habit. I wondered about Christopher for a while but his various 'substance' experiments didn't turn into anything serious or lasting. Anyway, I'm officially addicted to writing.

Clara's friend flew in this morning. She lives in New York, as it turns out. I wonder how those two ever became friends. I think, unkindly I agree, of Mutt and Jeff. As beautiful as Clara is, even at her age, as plain and ordinary her friend is. She comes across as a no-nonsense, practical sort while Clara looks more relaxed, always a dreamy look in her eyes. The woman is also sort of heavy with square shoulders barreling down the rest of her body, and the short, straight cropped hair doesn't flatter her pale, round, now sagging face. She can't be more than five foot one. She walked-in wearing pants and shirt, both of good quality but totally shapeless. The only shiny spot about her is a

157

pair of dainty golden earrings that represent some indigenous design, likely from New Mexico or somewhere in the Caribbean. For some reason, I think that maybe Clara bought them for her. To be fair, time sometimes wreaks havoc on some people. She was probably very attractive as a young woman. Then again, maybe not... Am I being overly critical or catty?

The two women hugged for a long time and you could sense the history between them. Both were holding back tears and laughing at the same time. Touching. I don't think I ever had a friend like this. I guess Richard is it.

Why didn't I ever make time to have real girl friends? All these women I played golf with, the parties, all those meetings at school, the pageants and concerts when the kids were growing up, the new graduates looking to me for advice at the firm. I was never close to any of them. I helped many during bad times but it was perceived as doing something nice for an acquaintance and no one ever imagined that I could be a close friend. Ok, I'm not much of a person to confide, probably because every time I do, things turn against me (read birthday) and gossip starts. I was told once that I intimidate people and it makes them afraid to get close to me. OK, this was from an angry teenager at home, but still, there could be some truth in it.

2 PM. Something really different happened. While I was near the front hallway discussing the details of tomorrow's shindig with the cook, who, thank god, agreed to cater the event and save me lots of headaches, a woman walked in and asked if we had a room. As it turned out, we did which is rather unusual for this time of year but for my kids canceling their visit. Anyway, this is our first walk-in, ever.

Her name is Patricia. She's a tall woman, someone my mother would have referred to as 'good stock', built to have a large family and live on a farm. As it turns out, when I walked over to greet her, I saw the business card she had handed to the receptionist and noticed the letters after her name identified her as an attorney. The postal address, however, justified my earlier observation.

Talk about not looking the part. But, here I am again, judging without knowing all the facts. She was wearing what appeared to be a new outfit, creases still in from the store package, and had very little luggage, the bag itself being a conversation piece waiting to happen. It was an old model, hard sides, the type that weights a ton even before you start packing. Looked like a relic from the 60's. Of course, she, as all my other guests seem to, appeared to be either in her late fifties or early sixties.

I mentioned that we were hosting an island party tomorrow night and that I looked forward to seeing her there. She smiled, nodded, refused help with her luggage and proceeded to her room, one of two on the first floor. I didn't see her come out after that, but she does have her private entrance, so who knows, she may be out there living it up… somehow, I doubt it. I hope everyone shows up tomorrow.

##

PATRICIA

"Remember the time we went to Myrtle Beach and couldn't wait to go home again what with all those kids throwing sand on our blanket as they ran by?"

Patricia was walking on the beach with Bill. He was holding her hand and talking about the one vacation away from home they had ever been on. She looked at him. Had she dreamed the last ten years?

"Well," he continued, "I hated it." He laughed and pulled her towards him, urging her to walk closer. "I never asked if you hated it." She tried to say something, but he silenced her. "What you thought you liked was what I liked."

He smiled and let her arm go. "Maybe it's time for you to find what you like. I have to go home now." She looked up to tell him he was wrong, she loved him and never wanted anything else in life but what he had to offer… but he was gone.

She woke up, lifted her head, uncertain of where she was. The sun had set and the night was dark. There was a dim glow penetrating her room from the solar garden lights near the door to her terrace, and running along the path. She remembered where she was and leaned back on the pillow. This was the first time since

Bill had died that he talked to her in her sleep. She had felt his presence many times, but never so close, never so real.

The bedside clock showed it was already past nine. She would have plenty of time to explore in the morning. She was a bit hungry, but didn't want to leave the room. She knew this was too small a hotel to have room service so she searched her bag and found one of the old cereal bars she always kept 'just in case'. Patricia opened a book and read until she felt sleep catching up to her again.

##

Part III

Friendships

JULIE

Julie was flitting like a colorful butterfly from the bar to the buffet table, eyes already shining from a first martini. Her guests were due any minute. She was getting very nervous. Apart from a couple of casual barbeques on the beach, this was the first 'real' party she hosted here and had no idea what was appropriate or not. A guitar was playing softly on the patio and the approaching evening looked like a promising venue for this event.

Christopher and Theresa would come after all, but later, once they had fed and tucked-in their brood. She was glad they had accepted her invitation in spite of its late coming. Her new dress, the one designed by her daughter-in-law, fit like a glove, her hair was perfectly styled and she felt ready to take on the world.

She spied Barbara and Grant coming in from the terrace, aiming for the open bar.

"Welcome to our little get together." Julie said. They smiled, thanked her and went to get some drinks. Then Lucy walked in from the hallway. She was wearing a colorful skirt and white top, an outfit almost flattering, Julie thought. She looked around the room and came straight to the hostess.

"I'm sorry, has a woman named Jackie arrived yet?" Julie smiled. "Yes, she has." She looked away from the woman "and there she is." Lucy turned around and greeted her friend with enthusiasm which, Julie hoped would become contagious. Right now, the party was very subdued.

Clara and her friend walked in from the terrace where they had been sipping tea, engrossed in a discussion which would not take in strangers. They went to the bar, and, Julie noticed, ordered sodas.

Betsy wasn't sure she wanted to attend the event. What did she have in common with any of these people? She was there to rest and was enjoying the native population to the point of wanting to spend more time with them then on the beach or talking to other American tourists. However, the owner had been so kind, she thought she's just make an appearance and leave as soon as she could.

Of the guests, Patricia was the last to arrive. She wore white Capri pants and a simple blue shirt. She looked around, smiling at random and aimed for the bar.

Jackie had also invited some neighbors and various other local business owners she had met at social gatherings. They showed up, fashionably late and brought the degree of enjoyment to a higher level.

Living in a small town and resort community, they knew how guests often had no interest in each other so they took it upon themselves to involve them in their own conversation. The tourists also offered some potential business for local shop owners so it was in their best interest to engage them in conversation.

Lucy and Jackie were soon conversing with one of the few men who appeared to have come solo. He was probably of the same generation but, in spite of a growing paunch and receding hairline, was interesting enough to keep the women's attention. Jackie couldn't help but compare him to Peter who religiously ran the entire neighborhood every morning, rain or shine, and had done so since she had met him. She thought she should consider herself lucky to have a man who didn't look like... her eyes went to a new arrival... this guy.

The man she was now looking at came in with a much younger woman, she estimated at least 15 years his junior. He looked like a project gone awry. Hair unkempt, shirt half in half out, baggy shorts, he walked in as if he owned the place. Jackie noticed Julie's look and thought this situation was becoming more interesting than the man Lucy was now exclusively talking to.

She separated herself from the couple and observed the new guests, taking note that both the owner and the bartender looked less than thrilled with their arrival. Jackie picked up a tourist pamphlet from a table and pretended to read while listening to the budding conversation.

"Good evening" Julie politely said, "I'm sorry Mr. Spencer, but this is a private party. We are closed to the public." The bar tender was keeping an eye on the situation and Julie, while still courteous and polite was interposing her body between the large man and the lobby.

"I didn't see any signs outside" he poked his head back to the door. "My wife and I decided we should get to know you better. It's just a coincidence that we appear tonight. A party sounds good, doesn't it hon?"

"Yeah, right" thought Julie. The man had been trying to sell her a bill of goods, literally speaking, accompanied by veiled threats about how hotel owners who didn't buy from him sometimes have unexpected problems. A real live bully.

She had seen worse in her career with the Wall Street sharks, so she always remained unimpressed by this little insignificant man and his mafia movie inspired self-importance.

This had been going on for almost as long as she had been on the island, but what with getting settled, learning the ropes, a wedding, babies, all of it interspersed by visits home, she had put him in the back of her mind, thinking that if she ignored him long enough, he would simply disappear.

Now, not wishing to make a scene in front of guests and friends, she kindly asked him to please leave, but he brushed past her and headed for the bar. His escort giggled. "He always gets what he wants." The bottled blonde, breast implanted, empty headed woman uttered while her surprised eyebrow line moved up as her eyes gleamed with admiration for her companion. "Excuse me," she said and walked into the room, leaving Julie in what would have been, under different circumstances, a fit of rage.

"What a guy." Julie turned and saw a smiling Jackie who had witnessed the whole interaction and was trying to lighten up the mood. "Yes, he's the town's notorious baddy. I keep wondering why the local authorities put up with this creep." "Well," Jackie replies, "there is one in every town. He's probably got them in his pocket. Hey, people like that keep us all on our toes."

Julie was shaking her head. "It wouldn't be so bad if he didn't take advantage and hurt people who can't defend themselves. That's what pisses me off the most." She looked at Jackie "excuse the language". Jackie laughed. "I'm cool. I lived in New York for a few years; I can hear or say anything without flinching."

Both women laughed and went back to join the party. After all, there was not much this man could do tonight except eat and drink his weight in food and liquor.

After finding out about her guest's background, Julie started talking to her about how she missed the city sometimes. Then the conversation turned to their former careers and they were surprised that some names of companies and people were familiar to both. They surmised that they had probably attended some of the same conferences or events thirty years ago.

This was an exciting time for both women who never had the occasion to tell stories and anecdotes about their past lives or share some of the crazy things going on in New York in the seventies. Julie was on her second Martini and Jackie, after assessing her current good mood, decided to have a glass of wine.

They walked onto the terrace and surreptitiously observed the 'crasher'. His woman hanging on to his arm and his every word, the man was now involved in a conversation on investment assets with one of Julie's neighbors. Paulo owned a small boutique nearby and had, himself, been harassed by Spencer before.

The poor guy was trying to get away without much success, so the two women looked at each other, smiled, walked over, and quite obviously breaking the thread of the conversation, dragged the victim away with them. "Thanks" the man said. "I thought I'd never get rid of him." He paused. "I don't mean to be forward, Julie, but why is he here?"

Julie rolled her eyes. "He just barged in and, in spite of my suggestion to leave, he just crashed in anyway. It was letting him in or getting a posse and chasing him out of town. I chose the first option in deference to my guests." They all laughed. "Jackie, this is Paulo. If you're going to do any shopping around town, he's the guy you want to know. Of course, besides my son Christopher who owns the arts and crafts place you might have seen on your way here."

The man shook his head. "You're too kind, Julie. I'm just a small merchant, trying to make a living for my family." Julie laughed. "Whatever." she continued, "he's got the coolest hand painted scarves I've ever seen and his line of women's clothing is fabulous." Paulo shook an accusing finger at her. "You're not wearing anything from my boutique tonight, although I have to say you look magnificent."

Julie twisted in a runway model fashion. "Meet my new designer," she paused and pointed to Theresa, busy helping out at the bar, "my daughter-in-law has many talents." Paulo was impressed. "I may just talk to her. If we could have a local designer with her own collection, it would be not only extraordinary, but also probably much less expensive than importing the latest fashions." He excused himself and walked over to the bar.

Julie smiled at Jackie and did a quick sweep of the room to make sure no one was alone or without drink or food. She noticed that Lucy and Dr. Hernandez were totally enthralled in a discussion. "Here's an interesting pair." She thought, turning back to Jackie and resuming the conversation. Jackie caught her glance. "Lucy may not look the part, but she is actually a very interesting woman. She wrote a book. In fact that's how I met her just a few months ago in a bookstore." Julie nodded and Jackie gave her an abridged version of the way she and Lucy ended up on this island together.

Lucy was having a great time. She couldn't remember ever laughing so much or feeling so comfortable talking with a man, especially one who was, for all intents and purposes, a total stranger. Her companion held her interest with stories about his stint with Doctors Without Borders as she told tales of her own bout with mission work in Africa. He seemed impressed that she had published a book and eager to continue engaging her in more subjects.

Clara and her friend were sitting in a corner of the terrace, talking softly and enjoying the extraordinary tropical evening. The music was soft enough so they could still hear the tree frogs as a background to the symphony of life. The women didn't share any of their moments with the other guests. Maybe later. But now, it was for them a trip back into a time where they were young and carefree. They were sipping on their soda but were high on the peace and serenity they had finally found here. Not too many words were exchanged but a lot was communicated.

"I'm so glad we could do this." Clara looked at her friend. "Me too. Thank you so much. Louisa was against it. She thought it would make me too tired or something, like I'm some kind of invalid." She smiled, "I'm only sixty, not a hundred." She paused. "Can you believe we've known each other for almost 30 years? Wow. Time sure flies."

Silent again, they looked over and saw that one of the guests was sitting by herself, looking uncomfortable and a bit forlorn. Her glass was almost empty and it looked as if she was deciding whether she should get a refill or leave. In normal times, either woman may have wished to take the stranger into their fold, but not tonight, not this time. They turned back facing the palm trees swaying over the sandy beach and Clara took a deep breath of fresh salty ocean air.

Betsy looked at her empty glass, rose from her chair and started walking to where the bar was, but also towards the path which would lead her to the lobby and then up to her room. She figured she would make the decision once she got closer to the mark. In her absent minded walk, she almost tripped over another guest. They laughed, introduced themselves and soon realized they were sharing the same thought: "should I stay or should I go?"

Patricia had only arrived the night before and wasn't sure about attending the party at all. Her chance encounter with Betsy was a blessing. She was glad for the company. "Where are you from?" she asked. "Well," Betsy replied, "now or originally?" They both laughed. "Either or both." "I'm originally from a small town in the Midwest, you wouldn't know it, but I've been living in New York for the last ten years."

Turned out Patricia did know the town well, a mere 20 miles from her own, so, excited to have this in common, the conversation went from where to how and why, then moving to the sharing of mutual interests. Patricia's involvement with helping the disadvantaged as a lawyer and Betsy's with what she called her humble work with people in distress.

Neither yet knew the other things they shared: both, under different circumstances and for different reasons, had been left to fend for themselves some years ago. Both had been rejected by the community they had grown up in. The two women refreshed their drinks and found a table by the pool to pursue their conversation.

Barbara and Grant were still standing by the bar, Grant leaning nonchalantly against it. They had been in the same spot since they arrived at the party two hours ago. "I'm hungry, let's go to the buffet." Barbara nodded and led the way to the buffet where the food, more like works of art, was displayed. The array of hors-d'oeuvres and sandwiches was set up in such a way as to remind of a tropical isle: fruits and cheeses surrounded the larger canapés and a sandwich loaf, in the shape of a boat, starred as the centerpiece. Grant observed and commented on how, as soon as the guests disturbed the esthetic of the spread, the chef would come and either replace the missing items or just rearrange the display in a pleasant manner. Another table completed the scene with desserts, almond and rum cakes and tarts surrounding another bowl of fresh fruits and petits-fours.

The couple each filled a plate, collected utensils and looked around for a table to enjoy their meal. They ended up closer to the pool where many of the patio tables were still unoccupied.

"How do you like your vacation so far?" Grant asked. "It's your vacation too" Barbara countered, "it's great. You couldn't have picked a better place. Thank you again." Grant looked at her. She was surprised since he rarely looked her in the eyes. He always seemed busy thinking about something else when she was there. He smiled. "You look good tonight." She almost fell off her chair. "Who is that man and where is my husband?" she wanted to ask. Aloud, however, she just said thank you. She was completely flabbergasted and could think of nothing else to contribute to this conversation.

Grant continued. "You know, you were right. Traveling is ok. Maybe we should do more of it." Barbara continued staring him back in the eyes. "That's it, she thought, something must be terribly wrong. What is going on?" But she couldn't say any of this. She just stared.

"I've been thinking. Maybe I should think of leaving my job, say, in five years or so. By that time you'll have social security on top of your pension, so we would be ok. What do you think?" Barbara's heart was beating so hard, she couldn't answer. "Barbara, what's wrong. Isn't it what you've always wanted?"

All she could do was nod and hold her breath so tears that started welling in her eyes wouldn't come pouring out. She nodded stronger and took her husband's hand. This had a calming effect. "Yes, Grant. This would be wonderful." However, deep inside she knew he still had five years to change his mind.

She shook her head, quickly dismissing this negative thought and made up her mind to just enjoy the moment, not knowing if it meant a new beginning or just this, a moment. Either way, she smiled and put her head on Grant's shoulder.

Back in the solarium, Lucy was still talking with her new acquaintance. They had a bite to eat earlier and were still sitting at the table, oblivious to the other guests. She was more and more enthralled with his conversation and surprised at how he seemed to find her interesting. Then her mind wandered and she thought about Rob and how different this man was. She didn't know they made them that way. She even imagined that her daughters would probably like him, and he would love the grandkids. She pushed these thoughts aside. "I've known a man for two hours and I'm building a life, just standing here, like an idiot." She concentrated again on her companion and let the wine lull her into a sense of well being.

Aware that they were both starting to feel the soporific effect of the wine, the man grabbed the glass from her hand, set it on the table with his own and suggested they go for a walk on the beach "nights like this were meant for walks on the beach." He said. "Every sound is clearer and every breath of air is like liquid gold." Lucy couldn't add anything to this statement so she took his arm, surprised at her own boldness and followed him out through the terrace and onto the beach.

There was a faint breeze, not enough to be cool, just perfect for brushing against bare skin like a caress. Lucy let go of her companion's arm, took her sandals off and ran to the water, enjoying the dampness of the sand, just freed from the last high tide. She had never, in her wildest dream, thought a feeling like this even existed. She was walking on air, in spite of the sand scratching her feet and getting between her toes. He followed her and led her on.

They walked in silence along the surf, enjoying this moment when all of nature's life forces meet in harmony. Some seaside huts were still alive with music and food but the couple stayed away from their artificial lights and plunged deeper into the dark recesses of the beach. They found a quiet cove secluded from human activity by palm trees gently sweeping the sky with their fronds. Lucy turned to face the large expanse of water, take in these new sensations and etch this moment in her memory. He then gently took her arm and turned around to face her. Without a word he just bent down and kissed her.

Lucy had never, in recent memory or even in any memory at all been kissed like this. His lips were moist and salty from sea mist and not pressing or overwhelming as had been her experience with Rob or as a girl in high school. He raised his head. "I'm sorry." He said. "You look so beautiful under the night sky, I just couldn't help myself." She smiled and offered her lips to him again.

He held her hand as they slowly made their way back to the hotel. No other words were spoken until they reached their destination. Looking at the time, the man apologized and said he had to visit a patient in the hospital early Sunday morning. With a brief, friendly hug, he left her standing in the middle of the floor, stunned and not knowing what to think. She decided not to try and just walked back out to the terrace to bask in whatever emotion she was experiencing.

Jackie had not had such a good time in years. These people were different from the crowd Peter took home for her to meet. They were real. They had lives that meant something besides making money and bragging about it. "Well," she thought, "except perhaps that Spencer guy." The man had fortunately left early in the evening. Even a cad such as he was, eventually feels uncomfortable where he is not wanted. However, she heard him tell Julie he'd be back the following week. She looked around, noticed a small gathering around the pool and made her way towards the group. Along the way, she came across Lucy who was just standing and staring into space.

"Hey Lucy, are you ok?" she asked. Lucy turned towards her as though she was an apparition. She then shook her head. "I'm fine. In fact I'm great." Jackie was trying to see what had put her friend in such a trance. She looked down, noticed the damp bare feet covered in sand and smiled. "I lost track of you earlier. You seemed to be enjoying the doctor's attention." She said with a teasing smirk. "Oh," Lucy paused, "yes, he's a real gentleman."

Seeing she wasn't getting anywhere in terms of getting a coherent story, Jackie dragged Lucy towards the larger group of guests she was originally aiming for and joined in a more lively discourse, one about comparative seafood analysis and the meaning of life.

Julie was keeping an eye on her guests, trying to keep everyone entertained, but noticed Barbara and Grant appeared to be having a disagreement. She walked over to where they were sitting. "Hey, can I get you a drink or something?" she said, pretending she hadn't witnessed the exchange between the couple. Barbara laughed and in a bold, unusual move leaned towards her husband. "Ok, you've come at the perfect time. We need a referee. Grant is tired and would like to go up to our room, but I'm still feeling in a party mood. What do you think?"

Jackie looked at them in turn. "I think maybe Grant should go to sleep and Barbara should stay with us and enjoy the party. It's not like any of you have to drive anywhere." She turned and winked at Grant. "I promise I won't keep her up too late and I won't let her leave the hotel with strangers."

Grant looked at the two women and shook his head. "All right. Don't come up too late." He said addressing his wife. "Good night Julie, and thank you for a lovely time." He squeezed his wife's shoulder, kissed her on the cheek and left." Julie was surprised to see the woman blush as if her husband's gesture was not expected.

By that time, most of her neighbors had left as had her son and his wife, and her guests were gathered around a table near the swimming pool. "Now, Barbara, let's go and see what everyone is doing around the pool and how we can get in trouble." Both women laughed and joined the group.

Clara was now alone while her friend pursued a heated discussion with another woman. Someone had brought up the subject of a recent pop psychology book, and Clara knew her friend's button had been pressed and she would not get her attention back until she had won or at least lead the discussion to its final logical conclusion. She smiled. "That's exactly how she would put it." She thought affectionately.

Betsy and Patricia were still slightly apart from the others, the two also in a heated discussion which was an offshoot of the one going on within the larger group. The women were pleased that they were with peers, people who enjoyed good, albeit sometimes controversial conversations. Julie had known when she purchased the inn that it would not attract the 'beautiful' people, looking to see and be seen. She was glad that after a few of years of trial and error it was turning into exactly what she had envisioned when she first glanced at the property.

Only Lucy was on the sideline, standing by the pool with a fresh glass of wine, under the spell of the ocean breeze, the stars and a man.

Julie asked for everyone's attention and signaled the bartender to bring drinks for everyone, all women now, left in the party. As soon as he was done, she told him she would take care of the bar if anyone was still thirsty and sent him home.

"Now ladies, if I may use that expression since I always thought I was more a woman than a lady, but this is all semantics after all. I'm glad we're all getting to know each other better and hope you're all having a good time. Now we can sit, relax and enjoy this perfect evening with our new friends. As you know, I'm Julie, I own this little piece of paradise and my goal in life is that you will leave from here with memories that will want you coming back for many years. After all, this is my nest egg, so it has be kept producing." Everyone laughed. "And yes, you guessed it. My past life was in finance and once a profit monger, always a profit monger!" she herself laughed and was imitated by the other women.

"No, seriously. As you can see from the name of this place, this is my last dream: I have crossed a major age decade recently and since I can no longer be a ballet dancer, join the circus, the army or the police force, adopt a baby or, probably get a job other than greeter at Wal-Mart, I may as well come here and live vicariously through my family and my guests." Julie raised her glass for a toast. "To all of us women of the world who have managed to survive school, puberty, work, family and all the men who tried to make us give it all up for them."

The women applauded the last statement, lifted their glasses and resumed their previous conversations. The mood was warm and festive. Julie was really glad she had decided on this party. Couldn't have been more appropriate since it appeared that her guests had so much in common.

Eventually, Barbara excused herself, and then Betsy and Patricia retired. Clara was asleep on the lounge chair and her friend gently woke her and helped her back inside.

Julie had seen Lucy quietly disappear earlier, which left Jackie, relaxing at one end of the garden, watching the moon reflecting on the water. Jackie was glad that, for the first time in over ten years the little wine she had sipped on all night had put her in an elated state rather than in the depth of despair. "Maybe there is hope for me yet." She mused to herself.

"Beautiful night isn't it?" Julie said softly as to not disturb this moment of peace. Jackie looked up. "Yes, it's miraculous." Julie hadn't heard that expression in a long time and wondered what the other woman meant. She sat in the lounge chair next to Jackie. "Do you believe in miracles, Julie?" Faced with a subject perhaps a little deeper than she could deal with after the martinis and wine chasers, Julie hesitated before answering. "I don't know. I suppose this place for me was sort of a miracle. I didn't know what to do next. Really, once you have lived so many years, sometimes you get to think there is nothing left to do."

"Yes. I know exactly what you mean." Jackie nodded for a long time. She turned and smiled at Julie. "Maybe this place creates miracles for those who come here."

The women sat side by side for a while, and then Jackie got up to leave. "Goodnight Julie and thanks so much for a great evening." Julie smiled. "Thanks I'm so glad we met. Have a good sleep. We'll talk again tomorrow." Both women walked away, one went to her room and the other cleared as much of the terrace as she could, said goodnight to the night clerk who had just walked in and went home.

##

BARBARA

Barbara quietly entered the room she shared with her husband. To her surprise, he was not in bed but sitting on the balcony, staring out at the night sky.

"Grant?" she asked softly. He turned around and smiled. "Isn't it a beautiful night?" Barbara walked over to the dresser where she kept the bottle of Port bought at the duty free shop before leaving the States. She poured two glassed, wished there were ice available, and walked out to join Grant. He picked up both glasses while she pulled a chair closer to where he was sitting.

"Did you enjoy the party?" she asked, not knowing how to deal with this new man whose head was resting on the back of the chair. His eyes had a faraway look she had never seen in her husband before. He turned his head and looked at her. "It was OK, I guess."

More confused than ever, Barbara decided to stay silent and wait for the cue that would dictate some comment or reaction from her. As it were, she was not reading his signals and was afraid to break the mood with any of the kinds of nonsense Grant just berated her for every day. They quietly sipped on their drinks, he, contemplating the horizon, she, wondering what she was expected to do next.

"What do you like best," Grant asked, "the ocean or the mountain?" Barbara was taken aback and felt cornered. She never thought of that issue and knew that whatever Grant would want whether to live in or vacation to, that would be what she liked best. She mused that this was the first time she ever voiced this consciously in her head. Thoughts of her experience ten years ago convinced her that this wasn't something she wanted to start. Having her own thoughts and ideas or making her own decision did not pan out to be so successful. From her parents dictating her behavior, and then putting her down for it, to her husband manipulating her into anything he liked, she could not stand independently and voice such an opinion, regardless of how inconsequential it appeared. She nervously said "I don't know. What about you?" She looked at him and searched for an answer he didn't appear to wish to commit to.

"I asked you first." Is all he said, and then smiled. Barbara wondered if the world was ending. This was all unexpected and most unusual. How could she respond and not have him put her down for whichever way she went. "Well," she finally replied, "The mountain is cool in a dryer sort of way and since you like gardening and cutting back bushes and such, this is probably the best place for someone like you."

She paused. "The ocean is nice too. You can walk on the sand and collect shells or sea glass. Well, you're not much of a craft artist, but on the other hand seafood is your favorite and it's total rest and relaxation."

She stopped, hoping he would pick up from there, but he didn't. He just looked at her again. "Which do you like?" he insisted emphasizing the YOU. She was out of ideas. She rose to refill their drinks and slowly walked back, trying to think of a safe compromise which would leave her unscathed. "I don't know. This is nice to be with you and not having to worry about frosts, raking leaves and warm clothing." She glanced at him to appraise his reaction, but there was none. "I just wonder if one could get bored in such a small environment, although I don't do much at home and haven't been bored yet." She added too quickly, turning again towards him for a reaction. Then it came to her, honesty was the best answer. "Grant," she said putting her hand on his arm, "I like wherever you like. I would be happy wherever you would want to be. That's my answer."

He took her hand in his and looked at her as though for the first time. "I've been thinking while sitting here tonight, why wait another five years, why not do it now. Retire. Get a boat," Barbara shuddered at the word, one thing she disliked in the world was boats. Sensing her reticence, he continued, "well, maybe not a boat, but a place near the beach. Maybe on the gulf coast or even somewhere in North Carolina. Or maybe a small country home somewhere."

"It would be nice to be closer to at least one of the boys." Barbara chanced to say. She noticed a sudden change in mood. Grant looked as if he had seen a ghost, finished his drink in one gulp and stared at her with what looked like fear in his eyes.

He turned his head, looked up in the dark sky with a pensive stare as if making an important decision. "I have something to tell you, Barbara," He then moved his chair to face her and grabbed both her hands. "I heard from Patrick last week." Barbara was surprised. He never talked to their west coast son, in fact neither boy ever called him; she had always been the go-between father and sons. She looked up, wanting to know more. "He called me at work and told me something he couldn't tell you himself and," he hesitates, "I got really angry."

Now she was listening closely. Patrick was such a gentle man. How can anyone be angry with him? She wanted to pick up the phone right there and then and make amends on her husband's behalf, but she chose to sit and listen to the rest of the story. Grant was very serious, sad almost, she noticed, and now hesitating to continue. He took a deep breath. "Barbara, Patrick told me he's getting married." Barbara took a deep breath, not believing such great news would be kept a secret from her while wondering where the anger fit into the picture. Grant held her hands tighter, aware of her pain and confusion. "He met a man and they have been living together for a while." Barbara was trying to swallow but found herself unable to do so. In a flash, pictures of her son visiting from college with his schoolmates, his never bringing a girl home and some of his unusual comments, came back to her mind and wondered how she could have been so blind.

"Oh." Was all she was able to say. "I was angry, Barbara, shocked and angry. I always thought he was different, but I couldn't deal with this." He hesitated then continued. "The gist of it is that I told him I only had one son anymore and hung up." Barbara's panic turned into disbelief. "He's our son. How could you say that? You always say family is the most important thing in life. What is wrong with you?" She had taken her hands away from his, surprised at her own reaction.

She had never talked like this to her husband. He sat back in his chair, surprised but sensing her deep feeling of anger or grief, maybe both. She wanted to talk to her son now more than ever. "I'm calling him." Grant held her back and sat her down again. "You're right. I was wrong." She had never heard her husband admit he was wrong. It must have taken weeks to bring him to this admission. Another thought came to her mind. "When did he call?" she asked.

"About two weeks ago." He confessed. Barbara had never been so furious. She did not remember feeling such low esteem for the man she had been married to all these years. Unable to talk, she just bent over, elbows on her knees, her head resting in her hands, trying to stop the flow of tears now streaming down her face.

Grant let her cry for a while, then kneeled in front of her. "I'm sorry. I was wrong. I thought about it all this time and wanted to tell you, but the opportunity never came. I should have told you then. I'm sorry. Usually, family problems can be solved just by waiting, but this one can't." She looked up and saw grief etched on his face. This was all new to Barbara. Even when his parents had died, Grant had handled the arrangements matter-of-factly without undo emotions. She felt sorry for him in some way. "Let's call him now," she said, "it's earlier on the west coast." He nodded.

They walked into the room and placed the call. Barbara talked first, telling her son how she loved him and would support him no matter what, then Patrick was crying and his mother was begging him to let them into his life again. Grant had his turn. His apology wasn't as sincere as Barbara would have liked but they were a family again and that's what counted. They promised to connect when the parents returned home. The wedding would take place in June.

The couple could think of nothing more to say to each other. They went to prepare for bed separately and slept facing opposite directions, uncertain about what lied ahead for them in the future.

##

JULIE

Sunday (the morning after) I just went by the breakfast room to see if all was back in order and, a quick glance told me the entire mood of the inn had changed. The women were sitting in small groups and there was a festive aura to the breakfast room. I'm so glad this worked out. Damn I'm good. Reminds me of when I used to close a big deal at work. I do miss that feeling, I admit, although at the time, I was the only one tooting my horn, so to speak.

I grabbed a coffee at the hotel since I got up too late and was too lazy to make my own. I'm so excited about this. Everyone is in great spirits this morning. I hung around just long enough to catch the 'good morning's' and 'thank you for last night' and came back here to my pen and paper. I did notice, however, that one person was relatively quiet compared to the others: Lucy. I saw her sitting with her friend Jackie but then, before I had a chance to pour my coffee and walk over for a chat, she excused herself quickly and went back to her room. I can see her now sitting on the beach under an umbrella, just staring. Hmm... I wonder if the good doctor... nah, can't be. Would be nice though. He's a great guy and while she doesn't look like what I think his type would be, who am I to say?

I overheard Patricia and Betsy talking about exploring the town sometime and maybe signing up for an excursion later this week. These two really hit it off. I'll try to talk to them if they show up for happy hour, just to see what these two women are all about.

I'm thinking that maybe when we reach a certain age, we need to find friends who don't have your past to judge you by. We're at the 'what you see is what you get' stage and don't want to be reminded of all our past mistakes... and lord knows there were a lot... at least in my case!

Insight: why is it that people very rarely remind us of our most successful moments? Seems like the bad stuff sticks around much longer than the good stuff. I guess it's just human nature. We look so much better when we consider all the dumb things everyone else does; also, if we remembered all the great things others did, we may be in a permanent state of despair at our own inadequacy. Something to think about.

I just got a 'heart sink' moment. That creep Spencer will be back. Short of causing him physical injury, which is very tempting, I don't know what I'll do with him. I think what kept him relatively low key since I've been here is that he thought I wouldn't last and didn't want to waste his time on a losing business.

Now, I guess he figured out I'm here for the duration and he's not likely to leave me alone anymore. Well… never on Sunday, like the song says. I'll figure it out tomorrow.

Ah, I just see Jackie coming around the corner. She's hesitating and I think she may be looking for me. I better go and see what's up.

10:30AM. Back to my coffee, now pretty cold, but still better than if I had to make it myself. I really like Jackie. Funny, my first impression when I caught a glimpse of her registering at the desk wasn't that great but now I find she has a great sense of humor and seems interested in what I plan on doing with the S guy.

We talked about having dinner together later. Should be fun, I'm really looking forward to it. The only problem about making friends with the guests, is that they eventually go away and then what? Oh well, at this stage of my life I'll take whatever I can get.

11 PM. What an evening. I just picked up a message from Richard. I don't think he's ever called while I was out before. Does that mean he's been lucky or that I really should go out more… something else to think about. He'll just have to wait until tomorrow.

Jackie and I went to my favorite seafood restaurant near the port and between soup and salad, we had the whole superficial story of our lives covered. Turns out she also turned sixty last year and appears to be looking for something or someone (??) to do with her life. She told me meeting Lucy and coming here were the best thing things that happened to her in a long time. I'm starting to feel like I'm running one of those reality shows. Where's the camera?

She also told me more about Lucy's book. I would never have guessed the woman would run away to Africa just by looking at her. I think that my years of bragging about how good I am at figuring out what people do in life, or what kind of persons they are, well, they are over.

We talked again of our times in the City and she told me about Bermuda. Not enough for me to gage how she really felt about it, but nonetheless... Turns out her husband Peter is in a similar field as Richard, but we didn't dwell on spousal discussions. (Why do men always think women talk about them?)

Our main subject was actually the S guy. OK you caught us, we were talking about a man. What to do? I don't know. She's only here for two weeks, so I doubt much will happen during that time... but I'm really enjoying her company a lot.

What a week this is going to be. Jackie was also telling me that she thinks Lucy is quite taken by our doctor. I hope she doesn't get too excited. I'm sure he was just enjoying her company and that'll be that. I guess we'll see.

##

LUCY

Lucy is staring at the ocean. She has been doing just that most of the day. She still can't clearly think about what happened last night. She's not even sure it was real. Earlier, she walked on the beach to get some lunch at one of the huts they had passed on their walk the previous night and ended up in the palm cove where they had kissed.

Daytime didn't do it justice. There were kids playing there now, building elaborate sand castles, women in tiny bikinis vying for a tan and restless husbands sitting on beach chairs, watching the world go by. The sight of all this vacation life took away the magical feeling she had for those few square feet of sand. She turned around, and made her way back to the hotel where the lawn chair with her discarded book gathering sand at its side was waiting for her to resume her post on the beach.

It is almost five and Lucy knows it's time to 'put herself together', shower, get dressed and maybe find Jackie or someone to have dinner with. She feels like she's abandoned her new friend, but she's sure Jackie is the type of woman who can find her own distractions. As she considers her dinner options, she feels a presence behind her. She turns around and there he is.

"Hi," the man says with a large grin. "I was going to come by earlier, but things got busy at the hospital, but I'm here now. I tried to call, but no one could find you at the hotel." Lucy looks at him not sure what to say or do, so he continues. "I'm sorry about last night. I wish I could have stayed longer, but, well... enough of me. How are you doing today?"

Lucy sits up from her previous reclining position and he can't help notice that a bathing suit does her better justice than the clothes she had worn the previous night. As most men, he doesn't see all the signs of aging Lucy suddenly attempts to hide with her towel. "Do you have plans for dinner?" he asks. She blushes. "Not really. I haven't thought about dinner yet." She lies. "Why?" "Well I know this cozy little casita not too far from here and I thought maybe you would join me. Yes?" She takes a minute to think about it and decides, why not? "Thanks. I'd love to, but I have to shower and change first."

He helps her rise from her chair as she wraps herself up in the towel and they walk up to the hotel. "I'll give you an hour and come back to pick you up then. Is that enough time?" Lucy laughs. "Plenty. I'll be ready." He waves goodbye and she floats up to her room to change.

She then remembers that the only decent clothes she has, she wore for the party yesterday. The kids gave her a bit of spending money, but she has to budget for food for another three weeks. She can't afford shopping for clothes. She doesn't even have a credit card. Her mood is shattered as she ponders what she should do. She wonders if someone would lend her a dress, but then faces the reality that she is heavier than all the other women here, except perhaps for Patricia and Clara's friends, but one is many inches taller and the other of a totally different shape.

Showered and preened, she stands in front of the closet where she stowed her meager wardrobe. The best she can do is a black pair of cotton pants and one of the flowered shirts she favors at home. "Oh well," she thinks sadly, "it was nice while it lasted… like a second!"

She's afraid to come down the stairs and tries to find some excuse for her laughable outfit. She told him about the book, but didn't mention that the pay was lousy and how she lives day to day, wondering if she will be able to pay her bills at the end of the month. This never came up in conversation.

She finally takes the plunge, leaves her room and goes down the stairs only to see him chatting with Jackie. Embarrassed at the contrast between her fashionable friend and her own ordinary self, she almost turns around to walk back up. Too late. She has been seen. She composes a smile and rushes over to where Jackie and her 'date' stand near the reception desk. "Good evening Doctor" she says, hesitating on how to approach him. He laughs. "Come on, my name is Juan. Forget the 'doctor'. I was just asking your friend if she wanted to join us, but she said she is otherwise engaged tonight." He turns back to Jackie and bows. "Enjoy your evening, maybe we can do this some other time." Lucy wants to crawl under a table and cry. She should have known he was not the kind of man to like someone like her. "Are you ready?" he asks.

Lucy nods and follows him outside, but not before looking back and catching an approving wink from Jackie. That sign of friendship and Juan's Smart Car parked at the curb bring back some of her confidence. "Wow" she exclaims, "this is really nice. I always look at those thinking that's exactly the car I'd buy if I could afford it." Lucy immediately thinks she shouldn't have said that, but too late. Now he knows she is broke. "I have a little compact that dates back from the Methuselah era." She laughs, suddenly feeling comfortable again, "I know one day it'll bring me somewhere but never take me back."

He laughs. "I remember days when I had such a vehicle. I should have kept it; it would probably be worth a fortune today." They ride in silence and in a few minutes find themselves in front of a quaint restaurant, where he is apparently a regular patron.

Lucy wonders how many other women he has brought here and how much prettier they must have been.

"Ah, Doctor Hernandez," the rest of the conversation takes place in Spanish leaving Lucy to feel left out. But Juan turns to her. "Senor Resendes says he has reserved the best table in the house for us." "Si, si" the man says, nodding his head, "We glad to see doctor with woman. Bienvenido Senorita." He extends his hand and Lucy shyly reaches for it.

The atmosphere of the restaurant is warm and friendly, but not really romantic. Lucy doesn't care: she is back to where they were last night, enjoying the conversation and being happy just sitting here. She even forgets her previous doubts and her questionable outfit. Her realistic self knows this is all an illusion, but maybe this is the gift she received from her family, a wonderful illusion. She smiles remembering the 70's Fantasy Island series. "Ok so I'm in one of them." And she turns off her worrying mind to make room for the happy glow of infatuation. She is confident that the future will bring her back to reality soon enough.

The dinner is excellent and crowned by the best fruit dessert she has ever tasted. When he suggests going to a local night club to hear a guitarist of some minor renown, she agrees without hesitation. A small crowd is dancing to what she assumes are love songs. She wishes she could understand the language and share in the passion of the story told by the singer and the weeping guitar.

Lucy knows it's late, but she doesn't want the evening to end. Juan eventually settles the check and they walk out into yet another enchanted evening. The tree frogs are out in full singing mode, muffling the sounds of the late night strollers. Juan drives her back to the hotel, opens the car door for her and walks her to the door.

She turns around wanting to say goodbye. She isn't ready for an affair or anything that compromising. She's never had an affair before and the thought itself while titillating is also scary. If he really likes her, he'll just have to wait. She has been celibate for so long she's not even sure why her post-menopausal self should even think of getting involved with a man. However, she can't deny the pleasant stirrings she experiences every time Juan is around.

Juan understands her body language and takes both her hands into his. "I'll drop by tomorrow night, if it's ok." Lucy blushes and can only nod in agreement. He bends down to kiss her and her legs weaken beneath her body. "Goodnight" she manages to say. He kisses her forehead as a last goodbye, waves from his car and leaves.

##

JACKIE

Jackie is sitting on the terrace after coming back from her dinner with Julie. "What a fabulous woman," she thinks. Is there anyone like this back home? She doesn't think so. Lots of nice, friendly people, wonderful she's sure, but no one with so much life and enthusiasm. She spies Lucy walking in and rushes to find out how her 'date' went. Her friend's eyes are shining and she looks as though high on some happy pill.

"So," she says "how did it go?" "It was great. We had a great time." Jackie isn't satisfied with that answer. She presses Lucy for more but the woman isn't ready to talk about it yet. Maybe in a couple of days.

Jackie recounts her own discussion with Julie, wanting to know if Lucy has any ideas on how to beat Spencer at his own game but soon finds that her friend shows no interest in the topic. She smiles and leaves Lucy alone with her thoughts, waving her goodnight as the other woman climbs back into her cloud and up to her room.

It's late but the evening just doesn't seem complete. Jackie walks up to the terrace where Patricia and Betsy are deep into a philosophical discussion. Not tonight, Jackie thinks. Restless and still excited about her conversation with Julie, she remembers it's earlier in the Midwest, goes up to her room, and picks up the phone.

Peter is home. From the tone of his voice, she assumes he was probably asleep in front of the television, but pretends not to notice.

"Hey," she starts, "how are you?" Surprised to hear Jackie's voice, Peter tries to say something more significant than 'fine'. "I was just thinking about you," he lies, "I'm very jealous of your lounging by the beach while we're still freezing up here."

Jackie is herself surprised at what she says next: "Hey, if you're so jealous, why don't you fly down and meet me?" Peter almost falls off his recliner. Never had Jackie ever suggested he could come along. He doesn't know how to respond. Is she serious or is it just an easy retort? How can he know the difference?

Jackie feels the hesitation and immediately regrets her question sensing his obvious discomfort with the subject. Calling had been a mistake. She just has to find a way to end the call. Changing the subject would work. "I wanted to ask you if you knew someone named Tony Spencer. Julie, the owner, thinks he's connected with some sort of mafia back home. His pastime is to harass local business owners and force them to buy overpriced goods from his import business with veiled threats and innuendos. I was wondering if you could find something out about him and let me know. We'd just like to stick it to him and anything interesting about his past or current affairs may just be the ticket."

Peter is disappointed at the turn of the conversation but replies that he will look into it or have someone at work do some research. They exchange some banalities for a few minutes and as they are ready to hang up, she says on impulse "and I did mean it when I said you should come." The line goes dead and Peter is left hanging on to the receiver as if it were alive.

Jackie settles in her bed, feet crossed, hands above her head, wondering what made her ask Peter to join her. It's not like their relationship has improved. Maybe it was just the fact that he knew, for the first time since they met, what she had needed most for her birthday. Ten years ago, he had gone along with her decision to fly to Paris, but this time it had been his idea. She turns off the light, gets up and walks to the balcony. She opens the door, breathes in the ocean air and listens to the surf gently rolling on the beach. She leaves the door open, hoping the night glow will bring the peace she needs to sleep in spite of the confused feelings filling her heart with doubts and insecurities.

##

BETSY

Betsy is smiling. Meeting Patricia was the best thing about this trip apart, of course from the local people she had learned to love. The woman impressed her by her sense of social justice and compassion. "You'd never know to look at her." Betsy thinks as she is getting ready for bed.

They talked for most of the evening and into the night about everything from senseless hate some people seem to have for anything or anyone different, to the laws and social mores that can transform women from victims to perpetrators. "There are no bad women," Patricia had said, "only bad laws." She confessed to stealing the saying from a T-Shirt she saw at a legal conference, but Betsy likes it. It says it all. She wishes she would have thought of it first.

She tries to imagine something clever which would apply to the many women she has encountered over the last ten years. Immigrant women, often in the country illegally, working for the very same people who scream the loudest in favor of sanctions against 'illegals'.

It seems to Betsy that if no one hired these immigrants, there would be no problems. She was never politically inclined and has no interest in controversies but she is aware of people's tendencies to "blame the victim". She also has problems imagining what people Jesus would have considered illegal and wonders if this cycle of hate will ever end. She says a short prayer asking for guidance in what she is to do with her future.

"Sixty years old," she thinks, "how did I get this old? No one warned me about this." She knows she will qualify for minimum social security in a few years, but one can't survive in the City on that. Living with the girls was not an option since she didn't want to be dependant and interfere with their lives but there would come a day where some younger woman would take over at La Casa.

She sighs and tries to imagine how the next decade will unfold. What if she got sick and could no longer work? What if she became disabled and unable to take care of herself?

She remembers her first few days when she crashed at Susan's, which now seems like so many years ago. She had glanced at bag ladies and reckoned she was just one step away from being one of them. She knows the girls would never let that happen, but still… she shivers at the thought.

The image reflected in the mirror hanging above the dresser is of a soft, serene woman who seems so 'together'. She smiles at her reflection. She remembers the make-over friends of Susan and Melissa surprised her with when she first arrived in New York ten years ago. The hair, the make-up, the wardrobe. The mirror at the time showed her a woman she had never known was waiting to come out. She had accepted soon after that this person was not really her but someone the world of magical theatre thought she should be. She was a frumpy Midwestern housewife inside, one with a perm and a bad haircut, using hair dye from Big Lots to save money. Or had Carl turned her into that hag?

Thinking about it, she realizes that the woman she now sees in the mirror is really Betsy, the Betsy she should have been from the start, should she have been born in a different family and in another part of the world. She still finds strength in her faith, but now blends it with the realities of life.

She turns to the open window and gazes at the lovely garden gently glowing under the full moon. The solar lights lining the path add to the shadows and create and aura of mystery. Her room does not face the ocean, but she can still sense the salty ocean breeze, filled with nocturnal scents and noises. Why worry, she wonders. Life would take care of itself. God would take care of her: he always had.

She leans on the window sill and smiles at the bright starry sky, something she rarely sees in the city. She sighs remembering all the loving souls she has met over the last ten years and can't feel but grateful for the gift of love. Then, she thinks about her son. The son she has not seen or even talked to in so many years and her heart swells up in her chest. Carl, named after his dad, same ways about him, but that never stopped Betsy from loving him. She never talks about him or her feelings to the girls so as to not upset them or having them worry about their mother, but he has been on her mind a lot lately. While parents can be forgotten or disliked, one's children produce unconditional love that never fades. "At least for women," thinks Betsy, remembering how many kids she had met who were abandoned by their father, some before they were born.

She turns and sits on the bed, thinking of all her loved ones who made this vacation possible and aches that she can't do more for them. Aches at not having reached for her son since his dad had died. "My world is perfect." She mutters to herself. "But a part of me is missing." She bows her head and without any words, imagines a prayer she should invent that would allow God to grant her a loving son again."

Betsy lies down, shrugging the negative thoughts from her mind. She falls asleep wondering how Patricia could help her with her work or, and this brings her back to full wakefulness, help her find her son and bring him back to the fold. She only mentioned him briefly to her new friend. Maybe the other woman didn't even notice since Lucy dwells so much on Susan, Mary Beth and the baby.

Sleep doesn't come easy after such an insight and Betsy has to resort to every common prayer she knows to finally fall into an agitated sleep.

##

PATRICIA

Now leaning on the railing surrounding her private terrace, Patricia thinks about all that has happened since she left her country home. Seems like it was years ago. This experience is totally new to her and, smiling to herself, she thinks she likes it. She has been thinking less about Bill and more about her own future.

She admires Betsy's passion for her work and feels a pang of guilt about her own social involvement. She knows it is a selfish way for her to forget her losses and fill the time rather than a genuine wish to help. This is a revelation. She had never questioned her motives before. It all seemed such a natural path to take, after years of working with lawyers. She had just followed it unquestioning, docile, as if a hand was holding hers and guiding her steps without any will of her own. Betsy had earlier looked at her as if she actually made a difference in the world, but Patricia knew better. She had no passion for her work, no affection for the people she supposedly advocated for, unlike Betsy who radiated love, serenity and commitment to her work.

"Maybe if I had kids it would be different." That thought brings back such painful memories that she quickly tosses it aside and replaces it by musing on her future. "I'm sixty," she thinks, nodding her head unconsciously, "what am I doing, believing my whole life and attitude can change?" she shrugs and decides this is just a phase produced by the enthusiasm of her new friend and the way she talks about the people she helps and works for. Patricia is confident that once this crazy chapter of her life ends, she will return to her secluded life on her little farm in the Midwest.

She walks back into her room and gets ready for bed. One thing intrigues her, however and she can't detach her mind from it: both she and Betsy have been raised in neighboring towns and this, in itself, produces a bond she has never felt with another woman. A friend. What a concept. She has successfully managed to shy away from any such ties in the past and cannot imagine building a friendship at this stage of her life. She smiles again and wonders what will happen next.

The women have made plans to meet for breakfast in the morning and take a tour of the island with a guide the next day. Patricia has been sensitive to Betsy's hesitation, likely because of the cost, so she made all the arrangements and pre-paid for the excursion. She hopes Betsy will go along and not try to chip in. After all, with no family, no one to support and in spite of the measly income she received as a part time court appointed lawyer, she has accumulated quite a large sum over the years. Since she has no plans for retirement in the future, where or who will that go to?

"May as well spend some of it now," she thinks before turning the lights off.

Sleep won't come. She thinks of all that has happened and remembers a book she read a long time ago. It was about a character who had to go through a series of passages before finding the treasure he was looking for. "Is this is happening to me?" she wonders. The impromptu exit from the snow covered countryside, to the edge of the Atlantic, then onto a cruise ship that took her here. Here, where Patricia knows something important has happened. Someone important has happened.

Wondering if Betsy knows the effect she has had on her, she decides that the other woman likely has many friends and thinks nothing of their exchange of ideas about their similar, but different, socially oriented work. To her, it's probably just a chance encounter of a like soul. Two ships in the night, so to speak. But to Patricia it is part of a new world that is opening to her, taking her away from the past and exposing a potentially different future.

She muses at how interesting life is that can take you to strange places where other participants, also in this place, have no idea how important they are to you. They are along for the ride and have no clue as to how every word they say or everything they do has such a huge effect on others.

With that in mind, she starts wondering if she, herself, has been a factor in other people finding their destiny. Court work can certainly cause life altering events, as well as be a factor in determining someone's entire future. Patricia feels something akin to a panic attack realizing how oblivious she has been to the degree of influence her work has on her clients: sometimes, it is almost life or death, prison and a dim future or freedom with a chance to start over. Bill hadn't been a trial lawyer and she worked with civil litigators at the time, so she has no way to know if other criminal attorneys felt as disconnected as she did.

Then there is Betsy. The woman's face keeps coming back in her now semi-consciousness. Her home, her work, her daughters and the son left behind, a son she hasn't seen in ten years. She only talked about him in passing, but Patricia caught a glimpse of pain on her face.

An idea starts to form in Patricia's mind, but sleep engulfs her and brings her a dreamless rest, her brain subconsciously focusing on finding answers to the questions she has raised. What should she do or where should she be after this journey ends?

##

CLARA

I just left Clara and tucked her into bed. She's not telling, but I know she's not well. Our conversations have been mostly about her life in London. I'm not sure she loves it as much as she dreamed she would. Tonight, she told me how she missed New York, but also confessed that the memories of the last few years are still vivid. She fears she would meet them at every corner should she return. Besides, she is far from independently wealthy as well as a practical woman who knows she can never find another apartment like the one she had under rent control. She is keeping the small settlement she got out of Claus to treat herself and her grandchildren to the occasional escape or gift. I insisted on paying for this trip as a birthday present, and now that I've seen her, I'm so glad I did.

I wonder how I will feel when I leave the city. I'll be alright. I believe I've used up my welcome and will be glad to stare at mountains and wild life for the rest of my life. The small farm I bought in Vermont will be perfect and keep me from losing my edge in a city that is not meant for older women like me. I would rather be alone than lonely.

I tried to convince Clara to come and live with me in my new home. She laughed. In fact, I hadn't seen her laugh so hard in a long time. She shook her head.

"Can you imagine me in a cow pasture?" she asked still grinning. "Where would I buy my weed? 'Cause you know I need it now more than ever." She hesitated and stopped talking. The smile faded from her face and was replaced by a deep frown. A wave of sadness came over me. First I thought she had given all this up after her rehab experience and her second cancer scare, second, and this is a hard one, I think Clara's cancer is back but she won't tell me. At least not yet. I think she's trying to spare me from having to be by her side again. If only she knew, I would die for her if I could.

Clara gazed at the ocean and started talking about how she ever got involved with Claus in the first place and the progression of the relationship to where she almost died. She had never been able to talk about it before. I followed her gaze to the black horizon and just listened. Turned out she had never given up the pain killers prescribed during her first encounter with the dreaded breast cancer. How a professional like me could not detect this, I'm not sure, but Claus had. She was the perfect victim: already dependant on chemicals, desperate for love and approval, and terribly lonely.

Shit, I'm crying. I never knew she was so lonely. I thought I filled her life the way she filled mine. What an idiot. What was I thinking all these years? Nothing, I guess, she considered me a dear friend who looked

216

out for her in spite of her sometimes erratic behavior, nothing more.

Strange how this manuscript has turned from a clinical analysis of a person haunted by personal problems, to what could be called a diary. Well, so be it. I am devastated that Clara may be sick again and I don't mind proclaiming it. After all, I'm now a retired psychologist, so my clinical analysis doesn't matter much anymore. I'm just a woman now, not much of one, so probably just a confused human person would be a more accurate description.

I keep reading about all the controversy over marriages between two men or two women and wonder what is wrong with loving someone, regardless of their gender? All my life I have looked at work mates and colleagues who built themselves little white picket fence lives while I was left to look in from the outside. No one ever wondered why I was alone. I'm sure they just thought that with a lack of good looks, it was only natural that no one would want me. Given my profession, I never could even live vicariously through clients who were often far worse off that I was. What a mess.

One person and one person alone knows my secret or knew, since she died a long time ago. That was my mother. I never told her, but she sensed I was not like other girls. Unfortunately, before she could help me out of the dark place I had cornered myself into, she died, a pointless death, hit by taxi while crossing the street to pick me up from school. I never had a father and the relatives I lived with, and then the foster homes just pushed me deeper and deeper into this dark corner. I never could find the strength to come into the light.

Out of your funk, woman, Clara would say. This makes me smile and I am now thinking of how amazing this place is. This is the perfect spot for our brief reunion. The women I met are incredible and, if I may put my professional hat back on, they are quite the homogeneous group in spite of their vastly diverse socio-economic backgrounds.

I always wondered why men often find it difficult to get along or socialize with others of different status, level of income or intelligence whereas women can find solace in almost any woman, anywhere. Is it a natural way? Women can all bear children and share secrets of unconditional love. Or is it a cultural issue? Victims of discrimination and abasement tend to rally together for support. Men, as the self-appointed superior sex need not find reassurance from others, but only allies to pursue their own goal since there are far less challenges and obstacles in their way. That could be why women shed more tears.

If I get bored in my retirement, maybe I'll research this subject and write a book. One of those pop psychology books someone was talking about the other night, the types that make the best seller lists. It may not even need to be researched since any topics relating to sexual differences will sell in spite of inaccuracies and made up facts. Clara would have fun talking about this. I'll have to bring it up tomorrow.

##

JULIE

Monday, 8 AM. I have taken to getting my butt in gear earlier lately. I'm not sure if it's because of my guests or just that I'm finally getting used to this lifestyle and don't need to sleep extra hours to remind myself of how relaxed I am.

I have also begun eating breakfast with guests. Well, actually with Jackie and Lucy with a wave to the other women (and Grant). That woman (Jackie) is fascinating. I'm learning more and more about her and was surprised to hear that she lives in one of those gated communities miles outside the city. As far as I'm concerned, those houses, all on an acre or two, are a step below the golf course homes in terms of nothing to do. She is such a vibrant, dynamic woman. I just don't get it. There must be something really wrong with her husband.

Lucy, on the other hand is just sweet and quite predictable. It's hard to tell if she's always been like this or just mellowed into it, but I suspect she's never been a firecracker type woman. I can see she is really taken with our doctor and hope this doesn't turn into a catastrophe. I guess at our age, any attention is better than none, no matter how long it lasts. I wish Richard was coming; I'm in need of attention myself! Oh well.

Most of the women are out visiting or shopping and, except for Jackie who has parked herself on the beach with a book, I seem to be the only one around. Clara and her friend left early this morning for a nature tour. They both look quite somber. I wonder what is happening there. I overheard some talk about a previous cancer, but didn't think it was my place to join in the conversation. Too bad. I guess one thing we realize as we reached this age is that we will die. Some of us have lost friends or relatives already and this number will increase exponentially over the next few years. Theresa's grandmother is now 90 years old and the last one left of a large group of siblings and friends who had grown up together, married together and now were all gone.

Well, too bad, enough dark thoughts for one day. What should I do? I find my personal contribution to running this place doesn't take too much input from me. With only a few guests and a great staff, I'm left with a lot of leisure time. I think I'll check out the computer in the office for a bit, make sure the money is well counted and everything else is running smoothly at the hotel, then mosey on over to Christopher and Theresa's to see my cuties. I'm not sure why, but I miss the family more than ever. Could be that the feelings of kinship and camaraderie I experience with my guests bring back memories of family gatherings and endless discussion at the dinner table.

Richard didn't call back and I didn't call him either. I don't know why. I just didn't. I should. I will. Here I go.

1 PM. I called Richard. He wasn't home and didn't answer his cell. Then I walked over to see the kids and found them also gone. I should have known, Mondays are slow and many shops close on that day. The family must have gone to visit relatives or just out on some excursion, although it would be nice if I were invited to these sometimes. Do I sound needy? I guess I am.

I see Jackie walking back from lunch on the beach. If she comes up, I'll catch her and maybe we can talk for a while.

3 PM. This was fun. We chatted about everything but the weather (what's there to talk about, it's always the same) and she went in to take a nap. That sun, if you come from a wintry climate, can wreak havoc on your system.

She said she saw a cute house that looks abandoned on the beach not too far from here. I know which one she is talking about so I told her the story I heard about it, or is it a legend, who knows? The house was empty when I moved here, so this is probably a third or fourth hand account.

From what I understand, some old woman lived there for like, ever, and every night, she would light the entire place with candles, inside and out. Theresa told me she knows one of her grandsons, or great grandsons, I'm not sure which. Apparently, the whole family cautioned the old woman about the potential fire hazard, her sons even tried to get her declared incompetent, but Doctor Hernandez who must have been quite young at the time, would not sign the papers and the judge, who also had known the woman all his life, refused to hear the case.

One day, and that's just what I heard, the sun set and a neighbor noticed the house getting dark and not a candle in sight. She walked over, noticed on the rail cap that the previous night's candle was burned out. She climbed the steps to knock on the door, but instead found the old woman lifeless, sitting in her favorite rocking chair on the porch. She was still staring at the ocean. Jackie said that's exactly the way she'd like to go. That was one interesting woman.

Why am I so restless? No more caffeine than normal. I can't stay in place. I tried to call home again and still no answer, then the office. No one seems to know where Richard is. When do I start worrying? Did I say home?

My worst fears are that one day, and who knows, it could be soon, I'll wake up and just become bored to death. What will I do then? I'm sure I wouldn't want to go back to the country club life or the financial world, then what?

This is the first time I even consider this since I moved here. Why now? This is my home and I love it. Why the doubts? Well, maybe hearing the women discussing their work, the difference they make on other people's lives or whatever relationships they have back there makes me feel that my life here is pretty dull. Ok, exotic in some ways, but still dull.

This is a very scary thought, one I wish I never had. After all I've invested in this life, pretty much everything I own plus many lost relationships back home, how can I even consider this not being my final dream? I even named the hotel "My Last Dream". How could I ever justify or explain that I simply 'changed my mind'?

Not going to happen. Just a phase, in fact, just a quick lapse in mental capacity. Ok, done, gone... boom... out you go.

I better get busy and start dinner. I asked Jackie to join me here tonight and, seeing that Lucy is already engaged in another date with Juan, she quickly agreed.

##

LUCY

Lucy looks out her window. Tonight might be the night. She remembers women talking about the third date being 'the charm' and shivers. The upside is that she can't get pregnant. She smiles, and then laughs out loud at the thought, but she's not sure she wants the rest of the hotel guests to know about any of this. Her room just won't do. In short, Lucy is terrified.

Rob had never been very imaginative and one other experience Lucy had in high school was nothing she wishes to replicate. She tries to remember conversations heard over the years, television documentaries on the subject, even movies depicting passionate encounters but draws a blank.

"And a doctor too." She thinks, imagining his success with hundreds of women over the years and then finding her, practically a virgin. How embarrassing.

She tries to put this out of her mind as she, once again, searches her minuscule wardrobe for a suitable dress. Those black pants seem to call to her again, the only item in the closet that isn't too grandmotherly.

"God," she thinks, "even my underwear is boring." She spots her black bathing suit and decides that this would make for a fine top-like shirt under her cotton white jacket. Maybe she can suggest the idea of a potential late swim as a reason for the bathing suit. Proud of the brilliant thought, she slips the suit on, then the pants and jacket. Perfect. Well, not really but good enough nonetheless.

Her attention goes to her face and she shakes her head. Not much she can do about that. What she needs but never knew she did, is a major make over. "I need a whole new body" she tells the woman facing her in the mirror. Shaking her head, she picks up her bag and heads for the lobby.

Juan is again punctual and appears just as she comes down the stairs. He looks amazing, Lucy thinks. She walks self-consciously aware of wearing the same pants as the night before.

A quick hug and they are off into the Smart car, but this time Juan drives away from the town. The small adobe houses become farther and farther apart and soon the Smart car turns into a side road and they start climbing the old volcanic mountain Lucy has only admired from afar since arriving here.

The road is narrow. There are hairpin curves and the woman isn't sure how to feel about this. This is her first experience of such road. She has nothing to draw on for comfort, except to glance over at Juan who appears to be comfortable, smiling to himself as if a bit demented.

Lucy panics. What if he is a violent rapist or serial killer? So Julie knows him. It doesn't mean anything. Julie has not been here that long herself and I don't really know her either. She starts sweating and her breathing accelerates in spite of her efforts to stay composed.

As if guessing his passenger's misgivings, the man laughs out loud and stops the car just as they navigate around a curve and reach a lookout point. Lucy is breathless. The small town appears below. In the dark it looks as if the stars are reflecting on the sand where hundreds of lights twinkle from homes and streets. The ocean is black with patches of silver moon rays. She has never seen anything like it. No transatlantic flight or domestic peak offers anything close to this vision. She turns and sees Juan smiling at her.

"Wow, this is," she hesitates, "breathtaking." He puts his arm around her shoulder. "I rarely share this spot with anyone. I come here when I've had a hard day and think maybe I should quit." He pauses, taking a long look at Lucy. "It's a very special place for me and I hope it becomes one for you."

Lucy is mesmerized, not only by the vista but by the man who drove her there. She isn't sure what comes next, but she doesn't care. It's all good. Her companion bends over to her side and places a light kiss on her lips, still in the wow position. "We can come back later," he continues, "now I want to show you something else which is dear to me."

The car climbs another, what Lucy thinks is a thousand feet, swerves into a narrow dirt lane and emerges in front of a large hacienda-style home, positioned exactly as to capture views from three sides of the island. She wonders if she will ever be able to breathe again. Her imagination brings her out of her body and into this panoramic setting as if in a dream.

"Are you staying in the car tonight?" Juan asks. Lucy blushes. She had not even seen him get out and walk around to her side. If he wanted to impress her, he certainly has succeeded.

She follows him up a stone walk lined on both sides with flower gardens which appears to have magically grown out of the rocky grounds. Solar lanterns mark the way. Lucy feels some relief in seeing another car parked closer to the house. While she trusts her companion, she is still not comfortable with what could happen next.

The house is all that it looked like from the outside, a miniature glass palace on an enchanted mountain. No need for curtains or shades. No one, unless flying over by helicopter, could peek inside those walls and at this altitude, the nights are cool and breezes from the ocean prevent the hot, tropical sun from overwhelming the occupants of this mountain jewel.

A young woman opens the door before the couple even reaches it and welcomes Juan and Lucy. He introduces her as Juanita, but Lucy isn't listening. She looks up at her companion. "Is this your home?" Lucy asks, still under the spell of this apparition. "It's really quite small," Juan answers, "but I like it. I built it on grounds where my parents used to take me on Sundays when I was a child. It's a very special place for me."

They stand, quiet for a moment, and he directs her to the dining room, small but made to look enormous by the outdoors blending into and enhancing the décor. "You have a beautiful home." That's all Lucy can mutter in her state of amazement. She never imagined people lived in such houses.

Now that she can spy into the rest of his domain, she sees that the place is, in fact, quite modest in size, but the glass walls and doors leave no room for feeling closed in and create a sensation of infinity of space.

She sits at the table and tries to regain her mental balance while Juan pours the wine. "I thought I would take you here. I rarely take anyone. I'm quite a loner and a very private person." He smiles and she nods in acknowledgement. "Thank you."

They eat in silence at first, then, as the wine is refilled, the lively conversation enjoyed over the last two night picks up and they are back to a comfortable place again. He takes her to the terrace off the living room for coffee. Juanita eventually leaves for her own home back in town. "She is the daughter of one of my patients. I hired her since they need money to pay for medication and other expenses and I am quite hopeless at housekeeping." He hesitates, "her mom has a heart condition."

The conversation wanes as they sit side by side looking at the lights below and the stars above. Lucy wonders where this is going or probably more how this is going to get going. She knows her role has to be minimal. She has no idea how to handle this situation, so she just looks ahead, hoping his first move will come naturally and put her at ease.

She tries to put a calm face on, but she is on pins and needles. After six decades of life, two children and a year in Africa, she feels like a 16 year old on a first date. Like that girl, she thinks that if they can get over this hump, all will either be magical or completely fall apart. She's not even sure which she wants to happen, she just wants this moment to be over, in spite the magnificent views.

"It's getting a little chilly out here," Juan said, breaking the silence, "let's go in, maybe I can show you the rest of the house." Lucy takes his hand to rise from her chair and feels like a docile girl on the night of her prom and probably the same weakness in the knees. They walk in and, after a brief look at a den, a guest room and bathrooms along the way, he introduces her to his bedroom.

Her heart is pounding in her chest. She can't hear a word he is saying, waiting for the inevitable to happen. The room is simple but large and French doors open up to the terrace. Even from where she stands, the view is spectacular.

However, this is one of the most, if not the worst, awkward moments of Lucy's life, she thinks, trying to calm down, standing there like a statue. Then it occurs to her that the doctor may be as scared as she is. That thought melts in her heart and she turns towards him. He smiles, looks at her and gently kisses her. "What do you think?" he asks. "Probably the same as you," she answers and they slowly start on the road which, to Lucy had been closed, she thought forever, many years ago.

The man is gentle and the woman timid. They stumble on the bed and clumsily perform a ritual so natural, but also hard when the advantage of impetuous youth is gone. The mood is broken by the bathing suit clinging mercilessly to Lucy's body, but they laugh, relax and kiss. "I was going to suggest a late night swim." She says sheepishly. The tenderness and soft touches almost bring the woman to tears, but she holds off and tries to reciprocate with the little strength she has left after what she could only describe as falling from the sky.

The sleep is dreamless and the morning finds them smiling again.

##

JACKIE – JULIE - LUCY

Jackie is up early, wanting to entice Lucy and maybe even Julie to accompany her on an island exploration trip. Dinner with Julie had been great. They had dug deeper into their past, adding philosophical discussions for good measure. Later, before going to sleep, Jackie thought Julie may be the only woman she ever felt an urge to tell about her Paris adventure. Not yet though.

She reaches the breakfast room but the only ones enjoying the meal are Clara, her friend, Barbara and Grant. The first two are having what appears to be a private conversation. As for the couple, Jackie wonders if they are on speaking terms at all. They both quickly add bite after bite in their mouth as if to avoid talking to each other. Not a situation she wants to be a party to.

She walks over to the flowery bushes separating the hotel terrace from Julie's private area but finds the terrace empty. She ambles back to the lobby after pouring herself a cup of coffee, wondering if she should eat alone or just forego breakfast all together.

Just as she is about to walk back up to her room, Lucy walks in, wearing what appears to be a man's shirt over yesterday's black pants. She catches sight of her friend who just stares at her for a second, then

233

breaks into laughter. "Lucy, Lucy, where were you?" she asks with a twinkle in her eyes. "Not here I guess."

Lucy smiles shyly. "That's not what you think." "I wasn't thinking anything, really" Jackie pauses, "but now I am. Let's have breakfast and you can tell me all about it." Past her first hesitation, Lucy, who never had such confidences to make, nor a friend to make them to, decides this is a good day for 'firsts'. She walks to the dining room and they sit as far from the occupied tables as they can. "I've already had breakfast, but I could use another cup of coffee."

Before the battery of questions starts, however, Patricia walks in and asks if she can join them, closely followed by Betsy who naturally sits at their table. Jackie loves the feeling of sisterhood, something she hadn't known much of over the years, but she really wants to know about Lucy's date. Afraid to make her feel uncomfortable in front of the others, she keeps her comments and questions to herself, for now.

In fact, it turns out that the other two women had researched the tours and Patricia knew all there was to know about how to find a guide and what was worth visiting. Lucy hesitates, not knowing how much the trip costs, but Jackie seems so excited, she agrees to go and take her chances that she can actually afford it. The group separates just as Julie walks in. Jackie intercepts her, wondering if she is interested in being part of their exploration tour.

"Sure" Julie says. "I'll do one better, I'll be your guide and take you around." Lucy, on her way up to change hears the exchange and sighs in relief. "I have to warn you though, I don't go up the mountain. We can get a tour bus sometime later this week if you want to see the island from a bird's eye view."

The three women meet in the lobby and leave for the grand tour. Julie has brought a picnic since parts of the island are uninhabited and there would be no chance to find lunch or even fresh water along the way. She urges them to bring their bathing suits or not since the beaches on the north side are secluded and rarely used by either locals or tourists.

The drive is quiet, Jackie and Lucy take in the views while Julie drives, trying to avoid chickens crossing the road and farm trucks coming around curves on the wrong side. This was one of the few times she drove herself around the island and remembers why it isn't part of her daily activities. Pretty scary, even on low ground.

Her concentration doesn't make room for much conversation but her companions are happy to simply enjoy the ride. Once away from the busiest part of the island, Julie starts playing her role as tour guide, and points to various areas of interest. She also relates some historical information about the island as well as whatever anecdotes or legends she has heard since living here.

After almost an hour, Julie slows down and turns onto a sandy road, leading to the ocean. The white sand is free of any indication that humans have ever trampled on its beach. The three women walk to the water in silence, then removing their sandals start splashing each other with the incoming waves. "I guess we won't be surfing." Jackie remarks as the small ripples barely allow for a knee high splash. "No, there isn't much surf here. Only a turquoise bed of calm water where fish can be seen swimming more than ten feet below the surface." The women ventured farther in the ocean and noticed minnows and other sea creatures peacefully going about their own business, whatever that was.

"Can I tell you something?" Lucy asks. "Sure" the other two women reply, Jackie hoping to hear about the doctor. "Being here has been a series of firsts for me, I have to confess that before landing in your hotel, Julie, I had never been in salt water or experienced anything like this. Thank you." "I didn't invent the beach," Julie says, not sure how to handle the other woman's gratitude. "Living on the east coast, the beach was such an integral part of my childhood, it's hard to imagine living a lifetime without." Jackie is itching to ask about the other 'firsts' but puts her curiosity in check until a more appropriate moment.

They walk along the surf for a while and find flat rocks that look as if placed there by nature so tired hikers can rest for a while. "This is just one of the hundred miles of beaches all along the coast" Julie continues, "and the amazing part, is that most are as pristine as this one."

Jackie looks up at her friend, "I wonder how long it will be before some developer decides to build time shares or condos and ruin it for both locals and visitors like us. So many paradise-like islands have been ruined that way. Wish we could do something to make sure this place remains human friendly, just the way it is.

They walk back to the car in silence and continue on their pilgrimage through virgin beach country, stopping here and there to admire the view, then for a picnic. By the time they return to the hotel it is well past 3 pm. The women take time for a long swim in the ocean, then a short one in the pool before parting.

Julie invites her companions to join her for a drink on her private terrace, but only Jackie accepts: Lucy is expecting Juan who will pick her up as soon as he can free himself from clinic duties and she is already getting excited about it. Julie wonders if she will give up her room at the inn while Jackie still wants to hear the details.

The two women are laughing and wet when they finally reach the villa and crash on lounge chairs. Julie is about to get up to get the drinks she promised when someone comes out of her house. In fact two people are walking out. The first, Richard, she knows well, and she runs over to hug her husband. As wet as she is, he just holds her for a while and returns her hug, lifting her off her feet for good measure. The other man, Jackie, of course, recognizes immediately. Peter. He has come. He was still listening, apparently. She slowly rises from her seat herself and slowly walks over. "What a surprise!" "A good one, I hope" he replies, a bit of fear in his voice. "Of course." She says as she gives him a friendly hug. Julie, this is my husband Peter.

"I sort of guessed," Julie says. Richard takes over. "You won't believe this, I was minding my own business in the plane when this guy starts telling me about a place where his wife is staying. Turns out it was here, so we came from the airport together and, well," he sheepishly adds, " we've been drinking to your health for the last couple of hours. Looks like you've been having fun too.

The women look at each other, shrug, and Julie asks Richard to get them drinks. The four of them, now around the patio table, stare quietly at each other. Jackie wonders what happens next. "Do you know," an excited Richard continues, "Pete here knows half the people in our Chicago office. Isn't it a small world?" They all agreed. "On a more serious note, Pete was telling me about a problem you've been having with some hot head here. How about that? How come he knew and I didn't?"

Julie pauses for a sip of wine. "I didn't want to worry you. It's really nothing. It so happens that the guy walked in on a little party I was hosting for my guests last Sunday and Jackie witnessed some unpleasant exchanges between us. I'm sure he's harmless."

"Well," Peter took over, "Jackie asked me to investigate for her and I found he's just a small time loser. Julie is probably right about his being harmless, but he did do time in Miami some years ago on extortion charges." Jackie chimes in "I thought he was creepy. That's why I asked Peter to look into this guy. Besides," she smiles "it seemed like it would be fun to rid the island of scum." The conversation continues with hypotheses as to the why, how and where the man comes from, but Peter is no longer being an active part of it.

He looks at his wife as though for the first time. He hasn't seen her with such spunk since, well, he thinks back, since never. This is the woman he first saw and fell in love with in Bermuda, but who disappeared the second time he met her. He is not sure how to respond to her. It's as though he is dealing with a different person. Having observed her over the last ten years, after her birthday in Paris, first in a morose depressed state, then in an accepting, sad, but willing companion, he had completely forgotten what Jackie could actually be like. A wave of sadness washes over him as he wonders why she is so unhappy when in his company and appears to blossom for others. What had he done wrong? What did happen in Paris?

Julie notices the look and wonders what is going on between the couple. While the women have become closer, they haven't passed over that intimate line that can take years to cross even with the closest of friends. She notices Jackie's mood changing as her husband stares at her.

Julie rises and gets some cold cuts, veggies, cheese and bread from the kitchen and they eat in relative silence. It'll all get figured out later, maybe tomorrow she thinks as the Jackie and Peter take their leave and head for their room. The men tired from the flight, the women tired from the island tour, both couples retire early.

##

PATRICIA – BETSY

The two women traveled everywhere together. Patricia had convinced her newfound friend that, if not for her, she would be on the beach, missing out on the most interesting sites the island had to offer. Betsy had therefore agreed to let her pay, as long as they kept it reasonable.

Both satisfied with the financial arrangement, the women proceeded to scout every remote corner of the island. Neither one was well traveled so they appeared to on-lookers as two kids exploring a playground for the first time. Patricia's experience, unknown to her friend, was beyond the exploration: she was learning to live outside her small box and was in fact enjoying watching her never used funds bring such pleasure to someone else.

Surprised at how they got along so well, they soon began talking about their past lives, Betsy touching briefly on her broken marriage without the details and Patricia talking her friend's ear off about her late husband, not mentioning the events which had led her to him. That was enough for now.

They are now somewhere in the town, sipping on ice tea among the mid-afternoon tourist crowd. "You know," Betsy says, "I only have a week left on the island. "I'm really going to miss you." "Me too."

Patricia replies. "But it doesn't have to be the end. I know we'll see each other again." She bends her head. "You know, Betsy, I have never had a real girlfriend in my life. This is very special to me; I want you to know that."

Betsy nods. Her friend knows she shares the feeling. "What happened to us? Why couldn't we be this way before half a lifetime had passed? We started from the same roots, but the paths we chose were so different. How does that happen?"

Patricia isn't ready to confide that hers had not been a chosen path but one she had to blindly follow hoping to find something better. Betsy thinks that her choices had stopped at 50 where something had mysteriously led her to where she was today. A wonderful place, but not the one where she imagined she would be as a young woman. They remain quiet, each woman following her own train of thought, trains that will maybe meet someday, but are now going in different directions.

"You never told me how long you plan on being here." Betsy inquires. "I know you just walked in, but what do you plan on doing next?"

Patricia looks pensively ahead then turns to her friend. "You know I haven't thought about it yet, but now that I'm finding that you will be leaving soon, I can't see staying much longer. Besides, Julie told me the hotel is booked as of next week, so I can't stay there anyway." She looks up at the sky as though searching for an answer, smiles and looks down again at Betsy. "You know what?" Betsy shakes her head. "I'm going with you. Yes, the more I think about it, the more it makes sense. Wow. This is so exciting." She then stops abruptly. "I'm sorry" she pauses and shakes her head," of course you have to tell me if it's ok with you first."

Betsy smiles. "Of course you can come along, but didn't you tell me you have a Miss Volvo waiting for you in Miami?" Patricia excitement turns to a frown. "Damn. I forgot about that. I'm sure I can think of a solution."

"I'm sure you can. But also," Betsy continue, "I have to warn you, La Casa doesn't have much room for guests. We may have to share a bed. But, I'd love for you to meet father Pascal, my friends and, especially my daughters and grandson." She was beginning to feel the excitement of her friend. "You're sure that's what you want to do? Don't you have responsibilities back home?"

Patricia shakes her head. "I cut down on my hours last year and on top of that, I haven't had a vacation day in all the time I've worked there. Worse come to worse, I'll just quit!" Betsy is shocked. She has never met anyone who could actually quit and not worry about it. She was more familiar with folks who lived paycheck to paycheck in constant fear of losing their jobs. "Well I guess if you want to come back to New York, I'd be really happy to show you around. Have you ever been?" "Never." Her friend answers, "I've never actually been anywhere except where I met Bill and the few places I glanced at on my way to Miami and from the boat." She smiles. "Pathetic isn't it?"

"Well," Betsy says, "I guess we're in the same boat, to pick up on your last statement. I took my first glimpse at the ocean ten years ago on Coney Island." She laughs thinking how looking at the water here almost made Coney Island not count. "Let's have a real drink to celebrate." She lifts her arm to get the server's attention and orders two Pina Colada's, "on me, this time."

When the drinks come, the women are giddy with pleasure and both secretly wonder how such a chance meeting may be leading to a lasting friendship. Both women are old enough to know that friendship is sometimes like love: you immediately connect with someone, but after a few weeks, months, sometimes years, the connection weakens and the friendship dissolves never to be revived again. However, neither one is willing to dwell on this.

They nibble on the fruits, playing with the colorful parasol leaning against the glass, sip on the velvety sweet concoctions and set off to find a sidewalk cafe for a light dinner before heading back to the hotel.

Once at the hotel, the women find a table near the pool to enjoy a cup of tea brewed at the bar and listen to the early evening sounds. Patricia excuses herself. "I'll be right back." She tells Betsy. She walks to her room and finds the postcards she bought when she first arrived and two pens. She runs back to Betsy. "Let's write postcards. I know it's not something people do anymore, and we may see the people before they get the cards, but, I don't know why, I just feel like doing that. Honestly? I don't want to explain anything on the phone, so that's a good way to let everyone know I'm not there, but I'm not dead either." She laughs.

Surprised, Betsy picks three cards, one for La Casa and the others for Susan and Mary Beth. "Betsy, you can pick another one. Maybe your son is still at your old address. What do you think?" With a sad look in her eyes, Betsy nods and starts writing.

Their task completed, the women both start yawning, laugh, and decide to call it a night. Betsy offers to find stamps for the cards in the morning since she is the earlier riser. Patricia will need time to locate some internet facility to make her new travel arrangements so she agrees and they rise from their lounge chairs and walk back into the solarium.

They hear some voices, turn around and see Clara and her friend come up from the dark beach. Patricia and Betsy look at each other and shake their heads. Something is not going well there. "Pat," Betsy says as they are parting near the stairs, "I'm so happy tonight. I wish life could be so good for everyone." She tells it softly enough so the other two women can't hear. Patricia nods and continues the daydream she had started to weave as soon as she decided to head for the City.

##

Betsy is in her room, still excited about, well, about everything that's happened. Her fears are that a return to reality will be a shock compared to this fancy life, but she misses her friends, her family and even the City itself.

She mentally makes plans to take Patricia to some of her favorite haunts and introduce her to everyone. Tonight, her prayer is one of thanksgiving for everything she had to experience for life to take her to this place. She just puts an addendum to God about Carl and hopes Patricia is right and that he will come around on his own. She wishes she could be that confident. She looks at the postcard she wrote earlier and hopes he receives it. All she wrote was that she missed and loved him and wished she could see him, but that regardless she prayed for him and wished him well.

Her sleep is restless and morning finds her at breakfast well before the coffee is even ready in the large self-serve urn at the corner of the solarium. To her surprise, her friend is already installed at a table, reading some magazine, waiting for breakfast to be served.

"What are you doing up so early?" she asks. "Well," Patricia looks up and smiles, "I had this excellent idea last night and working out the details in my head kept me awake for hours. And then I had to write it all down so I'd remember what it was this morning. I slept for all of two hours."

"What idea?" "Well," Patricia continues, "As you cleverly reminded me last night, I do have Miss Volvo in Miami and I really have to deal with her. So, I thought, listen to this and stay with me on that one before you say anything, we could both go to Miami." Betsy starts putting her hand out to stop her, but Patricia shakes her head. "Let me finish. There are actually two solutions. Both would take about the same time, but one may be better, first for my driving, and second," and she paused, "so maybe you could see your home town again."

"What are you talking about? I have to be back in New York. I'm sorry," she smiles as she adds, "but I think you're losing it." Patricia jumps back in. "No, no, let me finish. OK, you would need a few extra days of vacation, maybe even a week, but I'm sure you can arrange that. We could both fly to Miami, then drive back together to my home which is only a few miles farther than where your son lives." Betsy is now quiet. She has decided in her mind that her new friend has gone crazy. "Then," Patricia continues, "we could just find a flight to New York from O'Hare, there is one just about every hour, and you'd be home. What do you say?"

Betsy shakes her head. "I say you may be out of your mind. You're talking flights, drives, more flights; you're making me feel like a jet setter, which I'm not. I'm lonely for home now, I miss everyone and I really want to go back." "But you will," her friend says, "only an extra week, that's all you need. I'll take care of everything. I'll even talk to your Father Pascal if you want. Just do me a favor, come to my room and call him and your daughters and see what they say."

Betsy notes that breakfast is now ready. She walks to the buffet, fills her plate with eggs, potatoes, and fruits, pours herself a cup of coffee and walks back to the table. By that time Patricia is fidgeting. "Say something." "Just get some breakfast." Betsy answers.

No one in her entire existence has ever come up with such a peculiar idea. Her friend had turned into someone whom she shared a lot in common with, to some lunatic women trying to re-organize her life. Betsy was, in fact, a little upset at first and tempted to get up and leave, giving up on her new acquaintance.

Now, however, the more she thinks about it, the easier it is to envision how Patricia's idea could work. The idea of reconciling with or at least seeing Carl is also appealing. But she isn't ready to talk about it yet.

Patricia is back with her own plate and allows her friend to further digest what she has thrown at her without any warning. They eat in silence, refill their coffees and walk over to the terrace to enjoy the early morning sun.

Time passes, other guests walk in and out of the hotel. Finally, Betsy looks at her friend, pauses and finally talks. "What you said needs a little more explanation. I can't pay for any of this and I would never, ever accept any gift like that. But, you talked about Carl and," she pauses again, "well, you know it's important to me and, I may never have another opportunity to see him again." Patricia is holding her breath, waiting for more to come. "So, if, and I say if I can get the extra time and you can promise me that I will pay you back someday, it may take a long time, but I will, then maybe I'll consider it."

Patricia jumps out of her chair and gives Betsy a hug. "I'm just so excited. I know it'll work out. Don't worry about the expense. What you are doing for me is worth more than any money you could give me, but if it's that important for you to pay me back, I go along with that condition." She has tears in her eyes. "I told you much about my life but there is so much more. One day, maybe soon, I can share it with you, but now you are giving me a new chance at having a real life, one I can be proud of and share. Come on, let's make those calls."

They walk back to Patricia's room and, while her friend sits on her terrace to give her some privacy, Betsy calls home. First, she looks at the time and thinks Susan would probably be the easiest one to reach. Besides, she wants to pass things by her first as the most rational and unbiased member of the family, before approaching Mary Beth who counts on her for babysitting, and Father Pascal who needs her at work.

She dials the number and Susan answers on the third ring. "Hey mom! Is there anything wrong? We're not expecting you until next week. Where are you?" As soon as it is her turn to talk, Betsy begins explaining how her newly found friend thinks she should be going home, the long way around. At first Susan doesn't really understand the plan and bombards her mom with questions. When it sinks in, she remains quiet on the line for a moment, thinking about her mom, and some of the indignities she's had to endure for many years married to her dad, plus all the opportunities she, herself, had as a young woman that her mom never did. "Are you still there?" a worried Betsy asks. "Yes, mom, I am. I was just digesting all of this and you know what? I say go for it. You deserve it. What do you have to lose? I'll even send you some money to help out."

"No need to do this, really. But what about Mary Beth?" a timid Betsy continues. Susan laughs, "Mary Beth is now like a pig in shit, sorry mom, but she's ecstatic. When she met Francesca at your party, she saw how great she was with Alex, so she and Ben did some digging and found the young women has a totally clean record, only clueless parents, so, now your grandson is in the capable hands of a new nanny, thanks to you, and a young woman lives in the lap of luxury uptown where, if she wants, she and her baby will be well taken care of. Oh, and she's finishing high school at night. What do you say?"

"Oh God!" Betsy is crying by then, "I'm only gone for a short time and all that is happening. It's wonderful, I guess." "Oh, I forgot," Susan continues, "and because they found a nanny without any agency costs, Ben decided to make a donation to La Casa, so you won't have to labor with ancient kitchen appliances anymore."

Betsy is speechless. "Mom, are you there?" Now it's time for her daughter to wonder if the line is cut. "Yes, yes, I'm just in shock. Well I better go, Patricia is paying for that call and I still have to talk to Father Pascal and Mary Beth."

"Can't wait to see you mom and to meet your new friend. Tell you what, I know you don't have an ATM card, so I'll wire you some pocket money for the extra vacation time. Your friend sounds like quite a woman." "She is." Betsy replies. "Goodbye, Susan and I love you." "Love you too, mom."

Betsy walks out to the terrace, speechless. "Well," Patricia asks. "It's complicated, but, Susan thinks it's a good idea." Betsy plans on relating the whole story later, but now she just wished to get those calls over with. She quickly walks back in the room.

Father Pascal relates a similar story about Francesca, adding that the girl promised to come to La Casa on her day off too help with the kids or housework. Her family is apparently glad to have passed their problem on to someone else. He also tells her how much she, Betsy, is missed but that she can stay as long as she wants as long as she is back very soon. They are both laughing as they say goodbye.

Mary Beth is even more ebullient than the other two. "Mom, I love Francesca. You can go and do whatever you want, but I have to tell you, Alex misses you." She is silent for a moment and adds "Mom, say hi to Carl if you find him. Tell him we miss him too. But if you don't see him, remember you've got us and all you friends here who absolutely adore you."

"Well, Patricia, it looks like you have a driving companion." The other woman jumps out of her chair and hugs Betsy again, this time almost lifting her off the ground. "Not so fast. A few things you should know about me. I haven't renewed my driver's license in ten years, we may have to make frequent pit stops along the way and I am not a savvy flyer."

"Ok," Patricia says, dismissing the last part of her friend's discourse "planning time. I need to make a few calls, and then find some internet connection and by dinner, you will be in front of a 'fait accompli'. Betsy, I'll never be able to thank you enough. Now, you go get the stamps, then just enjoy the beach and I'll see you later for cocktails and a celebratory dinner."

The mood is festive as Betsy leaves her friends to do her errands. She walks over to the lobby, asks about where buy stamps and sets out to spend a great day, window shopping, talking to the shop owners and kids in the street. Maybe she'll buy some treat to share later at happy hour.

##

CLARA

Clara and I went for a walk on the beach last night and I finally got her to admit that yes, the cancer is back, this time in her liver and spreading to other organs. The doctors don't give her much time, a few months at best, more likely a few weeks. She refused chemotherapy and stopped taking any drugs besides pain medication. She is resigned. I'm not. I tried to stay cheerful but can't. I had to pretend I had an urgent call to make so I could run the rest of the way to my room. I don't want her to see my tears.

I know that every time I look at the mountain behind my new place I'll imagine Clara nudging me to grow marijuana for her. I can't help smiling at this. Hey, maybe I will grow some just to honor her memory.

I find it difficult to write anymore. I'm not sure I'll be able to continue this account of Clara's life and pain without letting mine show through. We only have a few days left of this vacation and I want to make them as special as I can for her. How can I do this? I'll just be with her for as long as possible and then say goodbye. I keep putting my pen down to think, but my eyes can't stop crying and my mind is dark and empty.

##

BARBARA

Barbara and Grant were living side by side, but had stopped communicating after their emotional exchange the night of the party. Every day, they sat on the beach, ate lunch and went through all the motions, but it was as if a knife had been inserted between them and any abrupt movement would set a stabbing in motion.

A few days later, they woke early and, as usual, had breakfast in the solarium, silence and heartache covering their table like an umbrella. They never communicated very much before, but this was different. This was not their usual tacit mutually agreed upon silence, it was a silence that weighed heavily upon the couple' spirits.

With only two days before going back home, Barbara wants this issue resolved before she explodes. Her thoughts are mixed and confused. She can't understand why Grant held such important information from her for that long. She can't imagine what is going to happen next. She only knows she is going to California in June regardless. She surprises herself in how, in spite of years of agreeing with Grant, she is now choosing her son over her husband. She thinks of her little cache of money from her retirement and is actively planning the escape.

After breakfast, they rise in unison as usual, but this time Grant heads for the lobby and walks out towards town. Out of habit, more than anything, Barbara follows him. People look happy. It's mid-week and the tourists in town since the weekend are completely acclimatized, looking relaxed and eager to shop or eat. Barbara has no idea where she and Grant are going, but she follows, not asking any questions. Those would come later and as far as she is concerned later is always better.

Her sandals are cutting into her feet and she has to slow down to remove the sand that has accumulated under the straps. Grant stops as well and waits.

She is wondering where the determination in his step comes from. He suddenly turns right into an alley and starts climbing some stairs leading to what Barbara now sees is an Internet Café. A coffee would be nice, but they have so many nice terraces in town, why here?

Barbara soon realizes there is no coffee, apart from some molasses looking brew with a donation jar sitting by an old dusty telephone. Her husband walks to a desk, hands some money to the man sitting there and aims for an empty cubicle. She follows, then finally breaks down and asks. "Grant, what are we doing here?" He looks up, but continued logging into his personal email account. After eyeing the list of messages in his box, he clicks on one link and settles in his chair. Barbara looks around and finds another chair so she can sit with him and maybe understand what he's doing.

"OK," Grant finally says, "you want to go to California, we're going to California. "But Grant," Barbara says timidly, "the wedding isn't until June. You have work." He stops his research and turns to his wife. "Barbara. How long have we been together?" He doesn't wait for the answer. "Long enough that I think we're worth saving and if going to California is what it takes, so be it." He doesn't expect any response. She always goes along with his decisions and this one is especially for her.

Barbara has never heard him talk about their marriage like that. In fact she searches her memory and can't recall any conversation that came even close to this. She nods, at a loss for words. She was always under the impression that she could have been any woman, or even a robot, and as long as the meals were cooked and the clothes cleaned and ironed, it wouldn't make any difference. And now, he wants to save the marriage? She decides to just go with the tide and not try to understand what is happening. She'll find out soon enough.

An hour later, after searching most on-line discount travel sites, Grant confirms a reservation, secures it with a credit card, logs out and turns to

Barbara. "Done. We're leaving the week after we get home. I'll take another vacation or maybe I'll just quit." He pulls his chair out. "Let's go."

They both leave the café, he, with a strong sense of accomplishment she, a bit scared at the new man she watched pounding the keyboard.

"Are you happy now?" Grant asks as they walk back into the main stream of shoppers. She looks for anger in his voice or on his face but sees none. "I think so." She bends her head. "I'm just not used to this. I don't know."

He points to a table on the sidewalk. "Let's eat." By that time lunch is going on full swing and the table had just been vacated by a previous customer. They settle down and, like the night of the party, he takes her hands and tries to capture her eyes. She is confused and afraid to do so for fear she'll do the wrong thing. He lets one hand go and tilts her chin up to where she has to look at him. "Barbara," he repeats his question, "are you happy now?"

She nods and tries to keep her eyes on his but remembers how their eyes rarely crossed except in an accidental, casual ways. She keeps nodding and he starts nodding as well. "Good. Let's eat, then we'll go shopping and we'll look at the duty free shops. There has to be something you'll like there."

The rest of the afternoon is spent hopping from one shop to another. At the end of the excursion, Barbara goes back to the hotel with a new silver bracelet and a dress she can wear later for the dinner Grant has planned for them in one of the best restaurants in town.

By the time they return to the hotel, everyone is either having a drink on the terrace or getting changed for dinner. They rush up to their room for a quick change of clothes and come back to join others crowded around the bar.

They notice that Lucy is standing arm in arm with the man they saw her talking with at the party. Now that the clouds have lifted, Barbara and Grant are both in a mood to celebrate and to everyone's surprise, start mingling with the other guests.

##

LUCY

Lucy is in heaven. She knows her time here is limited, but is determined to make the best of it. Her children were right: she will definitely write about this as soon as she gets home. The month she originally thought would be too long now feels too short. In the meantime she was erasing any trace of doubts or rational thoughts from her mind and enjoying every second of this totally unexpected turn of events.

She had another fabulous night with Juan the previous day and tonight would likely be a repeat performance. The lovemaking was nothing like she had imagined, seen on television or read about. It was more like a shared tenderness which made her feel worthy of his affection. She had never felt so selfish and selfless at the same time.

She thinks of Rob, a timid lover at first, who had matured into an insensitive husband. While they were married, she often wondered why he needed her at all and felt no better than one who accommodated his orgasm. She had even suggested once that there was no need for her at all, but he replied that her suggestion was perverted, adding that the problems was hers not his.

Advice columns Lucy always read in the local papers often had letters from men who complained about their wives rejecting sex after menopause. None of them evidently ever contemplated the real reason which was that they were just bad lovers, selfish with no imagination or empathy for their wives. This reason was never suggested by the columnists either. Blame the women, always. She shrugs those negative musings away.

Juan's hands were magical. Soft but firm, wanting to feel while giving pleasure. "Wow", she thinks "I have to write about this. No one will ever believe me."

She doesn't care. The days of 'sacrificing' for the good of who knows what, are far gone. Lucy has learned in recent years that the best moments in life happen like this, quickly, simply, often disappearing as fast as they occur. So, the key was to keep in the present and worry about the future later.

Everyone was in a cheerful mood around the bar. Even Clara and her friend joined the group followed by Julie and Jackie, now with husbands in tow. They all occasionally glance at Lucy and Juan with a knowing look in their eyes. Lucy smiles as Juan pulls her towards the door so they can start another evening of creating future memories.

Tonight, Lucy is wearing a new dress with matching shawl Juan offered her when they were visiting Paulo's shop. She is radiant as if the clothes, Juan or this very island has taken her to a new place and sensations she never knew existed. Life couldn't be better. They leave the hotel and drive to a restaurant with a terrace overlooking the port where lights from various boats reflect in the water. The seafood is beyond what Lucy has ever tasted. The night is all stars and ocean breeze.

"You are spoiling me." Lucy says with a smile. "I'm not the best cook on earth, but I think it's time I prepare a meal for you. We shouldn't be eating out all the time." Juan takes a hold of her chin and brings her lips to his. "I love spoiling you. You are a very unique person, Miss Lucy. I'll spoil you for as long as I can."

"How can a frumpy Milwaukee housewife with a no-class, ingrate ex-husband and no money to her name attract a man like Doctor Juan?" She asks herself. She can't figure this out yet, but for whatever reason she accepts the feeling, the attention and the wonderful love, for however long it will last.

##

JULIE

C an't remember what day this is, but I know it's 7 am. It's hard to get to my writing when Richard is around. Normally I'd forget about it, but this time I just can't.

Peter is interesting. Both he and Jackie have been hanging with us since the men got here. It's so rare to find another couple where both the men and women get along. Richard mostly couldn't stand the husbands of women I invited once in a while and I had major issues with some of the trophy-style 'bombshells' some of Richard's partners showed up with at various events.

The only couples who were acceptable to both of us were those from the country club. We played golf with them and organized dinner parties where all we talked about was golf. There was nothing else and no one to dislike or disagree with when the conversation stays on such neutral grounds.

I think Peter is a slightly distorted version of Richard. The biggest difference is how Jackie seems to, and I hate to say that, scare her husband. He seems to look for reactions on her face at every turn and for every word he says and that evidently makes her self-conscious. I don't know what goes on between these two, but it's a bit strange. I went shopping with her yesterday and we bought all sorts of extravagant clothes, even jewelry. I hadn't done this in years. The guys just holed up on the computer and discussed god knows what. They just seemed satisfied with themselves when we came back and joined them for drinks. Now that I think of it, I would say they shared and air of conspiracy. Hmm I wonder what they're up to.

The mood around here has been very festive. It is usually a happy place, of course, since guests are on vacation, but this uplifting mood is more than that. It almost feels like a family reunion rather than a bunch of strangers sharing the same walls. Maybe I'm delusional, but whatever, it feels good.

I saw Spencer yesterday. He was lurking around on the beach near my property, but when he saw Richard, he backed off and left. I never understood why anyone would think Richard is scarier than me. He wouldn't hurt a fly whereas I can be vicious, especially where money is concerned. Oh well, it's the old male thing. There are still some Neanderthals out there who still think 'he de man'.

Well, Jackie and I plan on teaching him a lesson. We're not sure what we'll do yet, but we have a couple of days to think about it. She's been reading the rather comprehensive report Peter brought about our Spencer guy. Peter hinted that he would like to prolong his stay, but the rooms are completely booked next week.

Richard thinks we could offer our guest room. I'll have to see how it goes before making such a commitment.

I'm so glad Richard decided to surprise me. Maybe spunk is something he is acquiring with old age. Whatever it is, I like it.

I've been neglecting my grandchildren lately, so busy with my guests. I'll make it up to them soon. Jackie and I dropped by the shop and she bought lots of stuff to bring home to her kids and grandkids. Toto was playing in his playpen and I found Jackie had none of the reactions women usually have with children, especially adorable ones like my grandkids. She complimented his mother but did not feel the need to talk to him, pick him up or communicate in any way.

She later told me she has problems bonding with little ones and is a hopeless grandmother. She's hoping to improve as the kids start holding proper conversations. And to think that all these years, I sometimes forced myself to hold babies, because I thought all women had to do that. In a way I'm glad I was wrong and that this is another one of those mythical female qualities that come, I now know, from nurture rather than nature.

Anyway, I'm not worried about this. Right now, I'm just savoring the satisfaction of a hostess job well done and enjoying the company of new friends, not to mention my husband's attention. What more can I ask for?

I hear Richard fiddling around with the coffee. I hope I can get back to this, but que sera, sera; I'll see what happens and go with the flow. Jackie and Peter are taking a day to visit the island and do the 'tourist' thing, so it's just him and me. Yummy!

##

JACKIE

Having Peter around on this vacation was an interesting experience for Jackie. She never knew him to get excited about much and now, he couldn't stop talking about Richard and some hare-brained idea they were concocting together.

She found him more affectionate and attentive than usual. They are now in the solarium enjoying an early breakfast before hitting the road. "What is it Jackie?" Peter asks. "What? Nothing." "Come now, I don't understand. Please tell me. We've been together, for what, almost 30 years? I think it's time you level with me and let me in on Jackie."

She looks at him and shrugs. "There is nothing going on." She looks at him, thinks for a few seconds and makes a decision. "OK, finish your coffee. I want to show you something."

As soon as he swallows his last sip, she takes his hand, pulls him up and drags him over to the terrace then onto the beach. Peter wants to say that he's wearing the wrong shoes, or even clothes for a beach escapade, but he feels this may be a breakthrough and goes along quietly.

The morning is magnificent; the beach is still deserted apart from a few sandpipers and sea gulls vying for the small crabs left over from high tide. After about ten minutes, she holds one arm out to stop him and the other to point. "Look"

Peter looks and cannot see anything special. There is a new house being built a little farther up, a fishing boat on the horizon and a variety of birds looking for breakfast. The only thing close enough has no interesting appeal: an old decrepit beach cottage with a green tin roof and wooden slats that appear to be rotting or, more likely eaten by termites.

She sees that he doesn't get it. She grabs his hand and walks him toward the abandoned house. She stops just short of the short boardwalk leading to the building. "Let me tell you a story," she starts. Then she goes on to relate the tale of the woman with the candles. "What do you think?"

Peter is puzzled, not sure what he is supposed to think and remains silent. Jackie continues, "I want that house." Now her husband is completely flabbergasted and can't help the look of disbelief and blurts out "did you see that house? It's eaten by termites and probably couldn't stand a wind over ten miles an hour. I guess it could be torn down and one could build a new house."

"No, I want that house." She says, emphasizing 'that'. Then she pauses and turns to her husband. "You wanted to know what was with me. You always try to know what I want, well, there it is." She let go of his hand and steps on the boardwalk to take a closer look at the house. Peter follows.

Jackie climbs the few steps to the porch and tries to imagine the old woman sitting in that chair, staring at the ocean, probably every day, often all night, and something stirs in her heart. She can hear the woman's voice, her spirit calling her to this spot. The rocking chair, now broken and damaged by wind and sand, is still there. She makes a mental promise to light candles on the porch every night to honor the woman when she moves in.

She really does want this house and standing on its porch makes it more imperative. She turns to her husband. He follows her but is afraid to climb for fear the stairs will just collapse under his weight. He sees her up there and can almost capture her aura. She fits the house.

Here is a woman, Peter thinks, who practically lives in a mansion, drives a Jag and she wants that house. If he were of another generation, he would shrug, smile and put it on a shelf, as an impulsive notion like all women have. But he's not. He sees his wife as he's not seen her before and wants to be part of who she really is. He wonders, however, if she wants him to be a part of this life or just the provider, as he has been for many years.

"OK," he says, "OK. I'll have someone look at it and see if it can be salvaged, then we can find out if it's for sale. "No," Jackie replies, "I just want it the way it is. It can be fixed a little at the time and look just like it did when this old woman built it." Jackie's hands are now resting lightly on the railing as she stares into space, a dreamlike look on her face.

"How do you know if it's for sale?" Peter asks. She snaps out of her trance and looks at him. "I don't. I just know I want it and I know we can buy it."

Peter is glad to hear the 'we' word. Maybe he can make that work. Maybe he can even make the marriage work. He was always there for her, thought he loved her, but now he wants to be with her. All these years of domestic life, the fear of losing her ten years ago, all are adding up for him to realize love is more than providing a roof, money, even food and he smiles when it dawns on him that he wants to grow old with the strange woman who is now laughing at him from the rickety porch. For better, for worse.

They walk back up to the road in silence and spend the rest of the day exploring and wondering how this is all going to work out. Peter takes a nap when they return and Jackie goes hunting to find Lucy.

##

JACKIE – LUCY

Just as Jackie was about to give up finding Lucy, she sees her friend coming back from the beach with her towel. "Hey, Lucy, hi." She motions her to one of the tables near the pool to sit with her. Glancing at her watch, Lucy smiles and follows the other woman.

"I've been wanting to talk to you for ages but between your Juan and now Peter here, it's been hard to find the time." Jackie starts. "First tell me about Juan. How is that going?" Lucy tries to adopt her friend's enthusiastic mannerism, but fails. "It's going well. I still have a couple of weeks left here, so I'm not in a rush to jump to conclusions."

"Do you think it's the real thing?" Jackie asks. "But then, what is the real thing at our age? I know you're not going to start a family." They both laugh. "You know, I'm a practical woman, Jackie, and I do wonder about what happens to new adventures like this at our age. One of us could end up having to change the other's diaper, or having to nurse a sick old mate for years. Can new love survive this?" She pauses. "I don't know, on the other hand, if I am to die in five years, say, would I regret not having jumped at the opportunity to enjoy some companionship over that period of time, no matter how short it was?"

Jackie has no answer. In fact she had never thought this far, to the time when either she or Peter would be sick, disabled, or worse, demented. She always assumed that her husband would run every morning forever and she'd be able to walk for miles until she died in her sleep.

"Lucy, I admit I've never thought about this, but don't you think just taking each moment as it comes is best? How many Juan's are there in this world?" Lucy laughs, "I think there's never been another Juan, I'm even sure the famous Don Juan himself wasn't so sweet. So, I can't answer that." "See," Jackie continues, "how can you say no to those feelings?"

The women sit side by side, thinking about all the intricate implications of growing old, although neither feels a day over thirty. "Maybe sixty is the new thirty." Jackie says out loud. "Yeah, think about it, when we were kids, the average ages were 63 for men, 66 for women, so a lot of folks our age just sat down and waited to die. Today, the odds are we have at least another 25 years to go, maybe more. Think about it."

"You're right." Lucy nods in agreement and looks at her watch. "I have to go and get changed for dinner." "Another 'date' I presume?" Jackie asks, in a mocking tone. "Yes." Lucy stands up but pauses for a moment. "Jackie, I'm so glad you came on this trip. I haven't been a very good friend, but it meant a lot to me. I want you to know that and also," she laughs, "to let you know that you are my number one fan in Milwaukee."

Jackie laughs as well. "Thanks but actually I owe you big time. I have found another new friend in Julie, but most importantly, I found myself here, and I'll let you in on a secret: did you notice the abandoned house on the beach just a few minutes from here?" Lucy nods. "Well, I'm buying it. Or, well Peter is buying it. I or, well, we may be living here."

"Wow," Lucy grabs her friend's hands then gives her a bear hug, forgetting about the sand and salt on her bathing suit. "I'm so excited for you. But," and Lucy hesitates, "didn't you tell me Bermuda was claustrophobic and you would never live on an island again?"

"I did," Jackie agrees, "but I am in a totally different place in my life right now. No kids to worry about, goals that include doing interesting, not necessarily profitable things, besides, Bermuda was different. As a foreigner, I didn't have the same rights as the native population. This is very understandable for them to maintain control over their economy, but for me it meant I couldn't, for instance, start my own business on a whim or become a consultant without a lot of hassle with permits, forms and other stuff which, at the end would likely deny me the opportunity to make a go of it. This place is different. It's not a country, but just a small island where rules dictated from the mainland are lax and from what I saw, creativity and new ideas are encouraged."

"Well, that makes sense, but that house you're talking about is totally falling apart!" Jackie laughs, "Yeah, that's what Peter said. But, for some reason, I really think I can bring it back to life and start lighting candles on the porch every night." Lucy gives her a puzzled look and Jackie has to tell the story all over again. While talking, she envisions herself on that wooden porch, writing the story for future generations to find. "That house is a treasure." She concludes in a firm tone.

They have been walking back towards the solarium and are now standing near the stairs in the lobby. They look at each other, smile and hug for a long time. "I'll miss you in Milwaukee if you stay here." Lucy says. "Don't count on it: first I'll be going back to visit, and second," she probes into her friend's eyes, "you may be visiting here even more often than you think."

There is still time left on their vacation, but their paths have taken different directions and for fear they can't say a proper goodbye when the time comes to leave, they hug again and climb the stairs to their rooms holding hands until Lucy reaches her own, and

Jackie walks in on Peter, still enjoying his late afternoon rest.

##

JULIE – JACKIE

The guys are inside on the computer again and the women comfortably parked on lounge chairs on the private terrace. "What do you thing they're doing?" Jackie asks. "I don't know. I just saw that they had been printing a lot of stuff on the laws of the land when it comes to regulating foreign businesses or people working here. In fact," Julie adds in a lower tone, "Richard told me he is seriously considering moving here with me soon." She confesses they were having an awesome intimate moment at the time, but she is excited nonetheless.

"How do you feel about that?" "Well," she concentrates on a bird flying overhead, and then smiles "I think it's awesome. The long distance thing is working well, but we find we miss each other more than we thought we would and he knows I'll never go back to live on that god forsaking golf course. So his options are limited." She laughed. "Either he moves here or moves here. That's about it."

"I have something to tell you as well," Jackie turns to face her friend. "We're buying the old house on the beach." Julie just about screamed. "How are you doing this?" "Well, I'm not sure, I just told Peter I wanted it, as is, and now. The rest is up to him."

Julie looks at her new friend. "I love that about you. You see something you go and get it. I wish I was less of a planner and more impetuous. The only time I did something like that was on my fiftieth birthday, but then that didn't last. I went right back to my well planned, well organized life. I have to say quitting my posh Wall Street job was a bit impromptu, but I think it was a long time coming."

"Funny you should admire this trait about me: it got me into more trouble, not to mention caused me to, not only screw up my life, but take a whole bunch of people down with me. No, I think you're the one with the right idea. Although at our age, now that all has been said and done, maybe my way is more fun." Both women laughed.

"Hey, what are we going to do about our friend Spencer?" Julie asks in a tone that says 'I really wish he would disappear so we wouldn't have to do anything.' Jackie smiles, "I confess, I have sinned, and you have my spontaneity to blame for it. I had a minute yesterday while Peter was, I hope, looking into buying my house so I paid the S guy a visit. Needless to say he was quite surprised to see me since our only encounter had been for a second at your party. Anyway, I had a packet of photocopied documents with me, you know, the ones Peter brought over, and I just threw it on his desk."

She laughed and paused with Julie's look urging her to tell more. "He touched it as thought it was dog shit on a hot day. So I told him to take a close look. I said I had researched the laws governing this island and that as a convicted felon in the US, he may be deported. This was kind of a lie, but I looked very convincing. I also threatened to go on a photocopying rampage and send this little package to the local authorities, who, even if they are in his pocket, could not ignore his past once the whole community knew about it."

Julie is now staring admiringly at Jackie, smiling and shaking her head. "That's not all," Jackie says, "I knew his wife was in the next room so I told him she and I could have a wonderful conversation about some other wife I had heard about stateside. I have to say this was the clincher. He tried to look superior, but I could tell he was shitting in his pants. So rather than hear whatever dribble he had to say, I continued. Ok, I said, now the conditions. You will not only leave my friend alone, but also all the other merchants you've been harassing and forcing to buy you stuff at inflated prices. Now, I'm nice, so, I will allow you to keep your business as long as you deal fairly with your customers and do everything by the book in terms of paying taxes and other legal issues. I also told him I would be here to keep a watch with your help of course." By that time, Julie is bent in two laughing and clapping her hands.

"Bravo," she says, "I just, I'm so," she can't find the words. "Oh," Jackie continues, "for good measure, I told him our husbands were closely related to many people within the US judicial system and could cause some problems for him with 'the long arm of the law'. I figured he's the type who is too stupid to know anything about this, so it was just a matter of intimidating him some more and bringing some of our guy's testosterone in the mix. God I loved it. I hadn't had that much fun or felt so alive since..." she looks up at the sky but can't think of when. "Well, since a very, very long time."

Julie finally has her voice back. "The local merchants will want to throw you a party, maybe even a parade. I know I want to. Thanks Jackie, you've made my day, and my week, and we'll see, but probably my year."

They are still in a congratulatory mode when Peter and Richard come out of reclusion. "Hey," Richard says, "let's go for lunch on the beach today, OK?" They receive no arguments from the women who quickly put a t-shirt dress over their bathing suits and the four of them start walking up the beach.

They walk past two of the food huts and the women are getting antsy, wondering when the guys will 'just pick one already'. But they keep walking. Just as complaints begin to rise in Julie's mind, the two men stop. They are standing in front of the old house. The women exchange a puzzled glance but remain silent.

Peter makes a grand gesture towards Jackie "après vous madame" he says in his worst French accent. "What's going on?" "Ok," Peter says, "here's the deal. The people who own the house are the grandchildren of the old woman you were telling me about. Even if they have their own modern beach homes, they have a huge emotional attachment to this place and won't consider selling it." He stops and watches the women's reaction, especially Jackie's smile turning into a frown. "But," and he pauses again. "Get on with it Pete," Julie impatiently says. "OK. The heirs may consider an offer, but they won't sell unless they approve of the buyers and get a promise that the property won't be used as a hotel or any other tourist attraction." Jackie is getting excited again. "No problem, we can promise that." "Yes," Richard chimes in, "but will they approve of you? That's the clincher."

That's when Julie smiles broadly and tells the men about Jackie's victory over the island's low life, Mr. S. "I'm sure once they hear this story they will give you an excellent deal. All these guys have some sort of business going on and have been victimized by this low life at some time or other." Peter looks at Jackie with renewed admiration. Now he knows what he had done to her all these years: planned, built, made money, never letting her be the only person she really was.

He takes her hand and they walk to the house together. He even climbs up to the porch while Richard and Julie look around the other side of the property.

Five of the grandchildren were delegated to see about selling the beach house. They are in their mid to late forties and are aware that the house will soon be impossible to repair. They also know their grandmother wouldn't want just anyone to have it. One, a banker wants as much as he can get but the others are more concerned with the conditions of the sale than with the price.

They all arrive in the same car and introductions are made. Julie was right, but what she didn't know was that the whole town already knew about her little visit to Spencer. The story, however, was different. He had told some of his customers that some lady had made him an offer he couldn't resist and they may have to deal with her in the future. This was one way for him to appear as though he was still in control.

Julie and Jackie were shocked. This is not what the deal was. Peter looks at them "Well, I talked to my partners back home and they may be able to buy me out." He turns to Jackie, "how would you like to run an import business." They all laughed. Jackie knows nothing may ever come of this, but the idea has her dreaming about all the possibilities.

The grandchildren ask questions, no money is mentioned. This will be decided later. Jackie walks over to the railing and looks out at the boat coming back to port with tonight's dinner. She answers questions, most relating to what they intend to do with the property all the while in a semi trance, with a smile on her face.

The owners leave Jackie hoping that something will be worked out with them. The two couples stop at the next hut along the beach and order a round of margaritas to celebrate.

##

Part IV

Starting A New Chapter

BARBARA

The decision was made. They would fly to California, then, when they returned home, drive north to witness a late spring in the northern parts of New York State and visit their other son. On the way back, Grant suggested they take her mother out of the nursing home in a town where no one knows her anymore and drive her back to Florida.

All is falling into place. Barbara doesn't know if the conversation about 'mountain or beach' will ever recur. Grant never mentioned retiring again after the night of the party, but Barbara is ready to take things one step at the time. She is going to see Patrick, her mom, then his brother and Annie and, who knows maybe a grandchild soon.

The couple is sitting at the airport, waiting for their flight to be called. Barbara is hanging onto to her husband as if by holding his arm, she is keeping him from changing his mind. It reminds her of a time when she used to take the boys to the supermarket: the stronger she held their hands, the less likely they were to ask for any of the shiny treats that often caused tantrums to erupt. She is willing Grant to stay that way with all her strength.

Her birthday isn't until September, but this is the best gift she could ever receive: to see her sons and, that she isn't so sure about, to have a husband who notices her as more than a comfortable shoe. Whether it lasts or not, this is more than she imagined she would ever receive from him, so she takes it for what it is: the best birthday present, ever.

She looks at him and smiles. He catches her eyes for a moment and for the first time in a long time a connection is made that requires no words.

##

BETSY – PATRICIA

It's all set. Betsy and Patricia will be leaving in the morning. Betsy was able to get some refund from her original plane reservation, so she planned on chipping in for the gas and travel expenses. Patricia has secured all the reservations, arranged for Miss Volvo to be attended to and waiting for them at the airport. She now waits for her friend to come back from town where she claimed having some last minute souvenir shopping to do for two families: the one at La Casa and the ones nature gave her.

In fact, Betsy received a notice about a money wire and was anxious to settle that immediately. She is sure Susan knows she has no money in the bank and was just being nice about the ATM comment. She is totally surprised at what she considers the huge amount her daughter sent her leaving feelings of guilt mixed with pleasure.

She buys a large bag of candies and proceeds to walk around town to say goodbye and give parting treats to the children she so enjoyed talking with during her stay. She also buys souvenirs and t-shirts from sidewalk shops and stops by Paulo's stores to buy two of his painted scarves for the girls and to say goodbye.

At Theresa's she hugs the children one more time and finds a beautifully carved wooden necklace which the young women tells her is an island symbol of good luck and long life. She buys one for Patricia and another similar one which she may keep, or give to Carl if she sees him on this voyage. She also finds a beautifully crafted cross set on a wooden base for Father Pascal.

The women say goodbye, knowing this is the last time they will see each other. "Julie is a lucky woman," Betsy says in Spanish, "I know," Theresa replies, "but I'm luckier to have her and Christopher in my life." They hug once more and Betsy leaves to walk back to the hotel.

Once there, she sees Patricia coming in from the beach, ready to pack her bags before settling down to dinner. Betsy follows her to her room and gives the necklace. "My daughter sent me a bit of money for expenses and when I saw this, the island symbol for luck and longevity, I knew I had to buy it for you." Her friend smiles and promises to wear it at dinner tonight.

Betsy climbs the stairs to her own room and starts gathering her belongings before dressing for dinner.

It is past six when they meet again in the solarium where guests are gathered for drinks. Betsy and Patricia notice that Barbara and Grant have already left and that Clara, suitcase waiting close by the door, will be leaving later for the mainland and an overnight flight back to London. It is a bittersweet farewell. Betsy hears others promising to return, but she knows she can't join in that promise. Patricia stays close by and they soon leave for a last dinner. They will likely never see these women again.

Neither woman knows what the future holds. For the first time in a long time, they are consciously choosing to take a road which may lead to serenity and happiness just as it can to disappointment, Betsy in hoping to see her son and Patricia, expecting to find a place where she can keep this feeling of being alive and be a source of happiness for others.

Only time and a long journey home will tell.

##

CLARA

Clara is leaving tonight. I wish I could go with her, but it's up to her family now. I was just glad to see her enjoying this vacation so much. I even saw a glimpse of the old Clara. I wish I could have done more for her, but I finally realized that this was the end of our line. It seems like such a load was taken off her shoulders when she finally told me about her health that she began sounding like the old Clara again, joking about how she planned on dealing with her inevitable end.

I told her to put sunscreen before going for a walk on the beach. She laughed at me: "What? So I won't die of skin cancer?" I was shocked at first, but eventually got used to her somewhat morbid humor. She had gone through all the phases of grieving for her life before coming here. I wish I could have helped through the others but found myself privileged to catch her in the acceptance stage. I went along with her jokes, finding some of the cynicism I used to love so much about her when we first met.

I have reached that stage as well. I'm no longer angry or in denial and have found that accepting life as it comes regardless of how short it is to be, is far more rewarding than wasting time trying to mourn the way we wish it had been.

Clara gave me a chance to talk as well. In what will have been our last conversation, I did confide in her and discovered my fears were unfounded. She had sensed my feelings all along, but didn't know how she could respond and perhaps help me. She told me the fear of losing our friendship was the reason why she never let on. She made me realize how much I had missed out on possible loves or relationships by stubbornly staying in my dark corner.

I have learned so much from that woman and wish she was around to teach me more. Even as I read some of my journal entries, I see how I always thought I was the one she should learn and get support from. I considered Clara a wonderful, but also frail woman. Now I know I wasted a lot of time: I could have learned so much more if I had only listened to her instead of putting her on a pedestal like a fragile doll.

I will be leaving soon as well, back to packing my books and following a new path, but the picture I had of my future has changed. Maybe there is still something or someone out there for me, even at my age and in my new remote pastoral home. My first goal is to rewrite Clara's story, showing her as the leading star of our friendship and the wonderful human being that she is.

My name is Sandy and I am no longer simply Clara's friend, I am a person who has hidden from my real identity for over sixty years, one who wishes that our friendship had been a love affair.

Sandy slowly closes her note book and pensively rests her hands on its cover. "Now," she thinks, "I have to start a new manuscript, one that will show Clara as the brave, loving woman that she is, not a victim." She stands and stares at the ocean looking within its depth for the courage to say goodbye.

Clara is slowly packing her bags. She no longer has even the smallest bit of energy and the effort she is making to do that simple task is exhausting. Sandy offered to help but Clara refused. She needs this time to think about how she wants to say goodbye.

She wishes she could write a note to the hotel owner to thank her, then compose a long letter to Sandy, telling her how she couldn't have made it through many parts of her life without her, but she can't hold a pen long enough, or coordinate her fingers well enough on a computer. She wants to write a book of advice so her grandchildren, especially her granddaughters, will not make the same mistakes she made, but she knows there is no time.

She is sad that her life will have been lived, with all the love, the pain but also with hope always raising its head at the end of each tunnel, and no one will remember. She wants to scream that Clara was alive. Clara lived here. Clara will live forever.

She sits to catch her breath and works at keeping herself from crying. What's the point? She wonders out loud. Then she thinks about Sandy. "It was always about me." She remembers their first meeting at the office where Clara had served as a receptionist, then, a few years later Sandy's return to the City, her cancer. "Yes, it was always about me."

This time with her friend was so special. She wishes she could have done more for her or given more than she had. She wishes she could express herself better so that Sandy would know how she feels about her.

Always looking like the wild one to anyone looking from the outside, she was in fact hiding how frightened she was inside. That's how Claus happened. He found that place deep within her, reached for the frightened soul hiding inside and used it for himself.

She shakes her head, trying to erase that part of her past which she is not proud of, the one that had the name Claus in it.

She wonders if anyone knows the guilt she constantly feels at having lived such a selfish existence.

Yes, there was a lot of hardship: married too young, having children she wasn't ready for and couldn't afford, being abandoned, but she knew there was no excuse for forgetting that others had feelings too. She believed many women cannot help being the way they are, but she could. She now sees clearly that she was one of the lucky ones who was surrounded by friends like Sandy and should have been able to make better choices.

Clara not only accepts her disease and death, she welcomes it. Life has been too hard over the last few years. Yes, her fault, maybe, but still she can't imagine taking that much more. Her only regret is that she will not leave anything that will keep her memory alive. Her only regret is that when she dies, it won't be long before someone says: "Who was that woman Clara something?" She knows her children think that her passing will be a blessing after all the suffering she went through, but it would only be if she left some of herself behind. It'll only take them a few weeks, maybe less to get over the grief: she gave them very little besides life, so they have little to be grateful for.

Clara opens the window, raises her head to the sky and, for the first time in years, prays that she lives long enough to tell everyone how much she loves them and how sorry for all they had to suffer because of her.

Her suitcase is packed. She looks around the room and proceeds down the stairs for a final goodbye.

##

JACKIE

"Well, that's it." Jackie thinks to herself as she starts packing. Peter is with her and they are both following their own thoughts. She looks outside and finds a few clouds on the horizon. That's how she feels right now.

She knew that things might not work out, but even when they finally did, her practical side took over and she agreed to go home, help with the sale of the house and pack the few things she wants to take back with her. She could easily have blown this off, but the thought of that letter in her vanity drawer was haunting her. It had to be destroyed and she couldn't take the chance of anyone else finding it.

The person she was when writing that note was not the same as the one she now sees in the mirror. While all the signs of aging have started to creep up on her body, her mind is back to a place where she can make a difference, make things happen, the only ways to keep her functioning and happy.

Peter has made arrangements for work to start restoring the old beach home and Jackie hopes she can move in by the time she comes back in a month or so. Julie has offered the use of her guest room but it wouldn't be the same.

The women are sad to part, but both vow to keep options open for new ventures and adventures they can have together on the island. Jackie has even faced Spencer again, asking him what it would take to buy him out. She thinks, probably not very much. Spencer resents doing business with the likes of Jackie looking over his shoulder and is making plans to set up shop in another unsuspecting exotic location where he can start abusing local merchants again with impunity. She knows that and is planning to use it in negotiations.

Over the last few days, Jackie and Peter have been hovering around their new home, trying to capture its mood and imagining how life will be once they become permanent residents. Peter is working out details of being financially able to set up some off-shore business and also work from here. In the back of his mind, he would like to see himself forming a partnership with Richard if all goes well. The need for information technology was growing at a fast pace even in this remote corner of the world. They would be the first to take advantage of it.

Neither man was concerned about the women, whom they knew could well take care of themselves. Peter reflected that perhaps for the first time since Jackie and he were married, she would be with him because she wanted to not because she had to.

Jackie was folding clothes on her side of the bed. Her thoughts followed a similar pattern. She looks at Peter and wonders how it will feel on the day when she doesn't need him anymore for financial support. The answer doesn't come and, like anyone who has lived that many years, she knows that only time will tell.

##

LUCY

Lucy's vacation is almost over. She thinks about all the other women who have already left by now, and wonders if fate will ever bring them back together. She doubts it. The whirlwind of new love is still in the air, but she knows she has to leave. She finds her plane ticket, passport and other official papers and puts them back in her carry on bag. Two more days until she flies home..

In a way, she is looking forward to the trip; she misses her family and can't wait to tell them about her adventures. Well, maybe not in details, but she does want to start writing again. The urge resurfaced a few times over the last week and she bought a new diary to write all she could remember about this month while it was still fresh in her mind.

She is torn between the joy of seeing her loved ones at home, and the pain of leaving the one she had grown to love here. Sitting in the lobby, she lifts her head from her diary and smiles as Juan walks in. "Are you ready?" She nods. As she puts away the book and picks up her shawl, he notices that she is wearing the dress he bought her what feels like a long time ago, but can't be more than two or three weeks. She is beautiful.

He mirrors her smile, takes her hand and they walk out into the warm scented evening. Without a word, he helps her into the passenger seat and drives to the casita where they had their first dinner. Senor Resendes is there again shaking his guests' hands and smiling as he walks among the tables. He sees the couple coming in the door. "Ah Miss Lucy. So glad you're back. I've heard a lot about you, now." Lucy blushes. "Our doctor here is telling everyone about you." His hand gesture suggests a broad spectrum of people. "I have a special table in a quiet, romantic corner for you."

They follow him into a cove, just far enough from the crowded tables to afford some privacy. "Gracias Senor Resendes." The couple settles in their corner and the owner brings champagne to the table. "Champagne?" Lucy asks. Juan nods. "This is our three week anniversary, a momentous event that deserves celebrating." He smiles and lifts his glass. "To the most beautiful and graceful woman in this room, and likely anywhere in the world." Embarrassed, Lucy lifts her own glass and takes a sip. Although they are separated from the crowd, she feels all eyes on her. She doesn't want to break the elating mood of the evening, but she thinks that it's also their last anniversary.

Shaking this thought from her mind, she examines the menu, but Juan takes it away from her. "Tonight is special, I told Senor Resendes to plan his most special dishes for us. No menu." Lucy looks around, but all other patrons seem preoccupied with their own meals and companions. "We still have two days." She says in earnest, trying to shake the sadness she feels inside.

"About that," he hesitates, "what would you say if I told you I bought a ticket to Milwaukee and will have a vacation of my own in Milwaukee?" Lucy is shocked. Milwaukee is not a vacation destination, at least not for someone who lives in paradise. She thinks of her tiny apartment and tries to remember how tidy she left it. She thinks of the bills waiting for her that she'll have to pay, the visits to the family, the writing she had planned. This is too much. How would he fit in with her dreary routine? Would she still love him once at home? What good could come of this? Her head tells her to quit while ahead, but her heart starts taking over and imagining them visiting the art museum, taking in a play or walking by the lake on one of those amazing spring days where all seems new and clean. Introducing him to Friday fish fries, freshly brewed beer, brats, all that is her home and that she has loved for most of her life.

Juan is staring at her trying to gage her mood. He sees shadows, reflections then the soft dreamy look he has come to look for and cater to. "What do you think?" She looks at him, searches his eyes for more information. "I would love for you to visit, but Milwaukee isn't anything like this. Spring can be nice, but also we can get some dreary weather. My apartment is smaller than this room. I don't know if you would be happy there."

She sees a wave of sadness cross his eyes. "Lucy, anywhere you are works for me. I would like to meet your family and then, if what I think can happen, maybe I can take you back with me after a while, for good." Seeing no reaction, he continues. "Let me tell you a story. I told you I was married once and you never asked about it. Well, we met in college when I was in Medical School and she was just about to graduate with a business degree." He smiles. "This was many years ago, but I remember how much we enjoyed each other, just as you and I did the past few weeks."

He pauses to allow the server to refresh their drinks. "We married after her graduation but decided to wait until my residency was over to have children. When I finally made it through, we moved in a larger apartment and she got pregnant." Lucy lifts her eyebrows. She had no idea.

"Yes, but before we had a chance to enjoy this part of our lives, Elsa, her name was Elsa, was in a car crash, lost the baby and died after a month in a coma. I was devastated and couldn't stay in the States. Too many memories. That's when I joined Doctors Without Borders and eventually came back home to start a practice in town." He stops and looks down on the table as if his thoughts are getting mixed up with the salad Senor Resendes is serving them.

Lucy looks at him and sees the pain time has obviously never erased. "I had no idea." Juan regains his composure. "Anyway, when I saw you, I felt that same connection and now, I just can't let you go." He hesitates, "I love you Lucy." She can see fear in his eyes now, fear of rejection, fear of losing her. "I love you too, Juan." She hesitates, "but this is so new. How do we know it will last?"

Juan shakes his head, "we won't know unless we stay together, no matter where, no matter what. That's why I would like to fly home with you so we can explore these feelings and decide on what we should do about them." He pauses, 'I promise you that I will leave the minute you ask me, no questions asked."

"You know, Juan, my heart tells me it wants you around for a very long time, but my head cannot imagine you living up north, nor me living here all year." He nods. "I've thought about this too. You know I'm a bit older than you, so maybe it's time I start thinking about retirement or at least cutting back on hours. So we could share our time between your world and mine. But hey, let's just try it. What have we got to lose?"

Lucy knows that what they have to lose is each other and the fond memories of their three weeks in paradise, but she remains silent. She even smiles, thinking that her new book will need a proper ending whether it is favorable or not, so, she looks in his eyes again. "Why not? Let's do this." Juan takes her hand, relieved, and just says "thank you."

That night, after Juan falls asleep, Lucy writes in her diary. "Tonight, I made a decision that may change my life. But at 60, if there is still the hint of a possibility to live new adventures and find love, who am I to say no?"

She puts the pen down, lies back on the pillow, takes Juan's sleeping hand in hers and smiles.

##

JULIE

8 AM. Everyone has left. New guests are filling the rooms and I hope their lives improve because of having been here. Sounds corny, but I now half expect Tattoo to climb on some tower and scream "De Plane, De Plane" When new guests arrive.

I just now realize how much I need to be part of a community, of a group of people with different opinions or ideas but with whom I still have a lot in common. Wow, that's heavy... at least for 8 AM.

I'm so excited. Richard is definitely coming to live here permanently at around the same time when Jake finishes school in May. He'll be operating a satellite office and leave clients' contact to his colleagues. We're hoping to have sold 'the big house' by then and built an office here for Richard to work in. I suspect he and Peter are concocting some talent merger and a way to claim independence from the rat race, but nothing concrete yet.

Just think, by summer I'll have two of my children around and my husband here for good. All I need is for Josée to decide to set up a dental practice at the local clinic and we'll have a family again. Wow. I'm still in shock. Jake will have to go to boarding school next year, but then I'll have him here for every holiday and vacation. We haven't told him or Josée about any of this yet, Richard wanted to do it in person, but I'm sure they'll be ok with his decision. I'm already envisioning a spring break party here with Jake's friends and, of course, me as chaperon. I may be setting myself up for disappointment, but I'm feeling so good, I'm just going to take things as they come and be, as politicians say, cautiously optimistic.

I just talked to Jackie and she's expecting to move to her beach house at about the same time. She has all sorts of ideas, but I suspect she'll just want to enjoy the stress free lifestyle before getting involved in a business. I never believed I could find such a friend at this stage of my life. I always thought that friends were long time in the making, fragile, needing nurturing and often fleeting. But I was wrong, or at least we'll see. Before our friendship is carved in stone, we'll likely have to go through some difficult times together. Saying there will never be any would be a total denial of how the real world works. However those times are what bring a friendship (and often even a marriage) to either a higher level or a separation.

Not sure what Betsy and Patricia will come up with, but I believe that they too have discovered life can be unpredictable and the best thing is to go with the flow. It's quite the trek they started on. If they can still be friends after being in a car together for over a thousand miles, I'll be impressed. Unfortunately, I will likely never find out. This is the downside of this business: you just start knowing your guests and then they leave, most, if not all, never to be seen or heard from again. I guess it's like life but multiplied by an exponential number. I was told that eventually, you learn to separate yourself from your business and only maintain the relationship with guests as a business proposition. I tried that for the first while, but, after the last few weeks, I'm not sure I'll ever be able to do it again. If one works at a Hilton, that may be possible, but in this small inn, I don't think so.

Just had a thought… maybe I can start a 'Same Time Next Year' club, so I'll get to see those guests at least once a year, not to mention guarantee myself a steady income. (How crass of me, I'm ashamed). Nonetheless, an interesting concept. I'll have to mention it to Jackie when she comes back.

As for Lucy, it's all in the balance now. This romance was built on sand and sun. Can it stand the harsh climates and the reality that will fall upon them once they land in Wisconsin? Who knows? The upside is, I will know the outcome of that one regardless of how much time it takes to develop: I know our good doctor will be back and Jackie will keep track of Lucy. Something to look forward to, I guess.

I was going to write about wishing them luck, but what would luck be in this case? That she leaves her home and family for him? That he leaves his

patients and mountain perch for her? I don't know.
How much can two people compromise on lifelong
commitments and family ties? Life never ceases to
offer these circular dilemmas.

I can barely talk about Clara and Sandy. Such a
sad story. I don't know all the details; I know there was
much more to it that they never shared with us. I had to
stop before writing the next part. Clara will die, maybe
next week or next month, her fate is sealed. How can
that possibly feel?

Watching Clara painfully get into the taxi and
her friend being so attentive just broke my heart. I only
heard her friend say that she would keep her memory
alive forever. Sandy left a few days later, but never
came for afternoon tea or cocktail hour. She just spent
her last few days on the beach, writing in her note book
and just smiling when someone else passed by. I
suspect she also learned a lot about herself on this trip.
How to be the one left behind is one of those lessons. I
shudder to even think about how and when I'll have to
be in such a position.

I wonder if I will find out when Clara's life ends.
Probably not. We were, as the old saying goes, 'ships
crossing in the night'. I will remember these women for
a long time and hope that Sandy finds some solace
once she settles on her farm. I wish I could hope she
finds love.

Mr. and Mrs. as my staff originally coined the couple finally became Barbara and Grant by the time they left. Another minor miracle of two people together for decades who finally connect and wake up to enjoy the few years they have left.

I'm not supposed to know that, but I did overhear one of their conversations at breakfast, about their son in California and was really glad when they said that they would make the rounds of visits to both the east and west coasts after they got back to the States.

Unlike Jackie who jumped into open doors and opportunities, I always used to have strategies and procedures for every inch of my future. Since I've been here, the closest I get to planning is when I walk on the beach and daydream about what I would like to happen next.

It took six decades of life to finally understand my mom's favorite saying which I know now is true that: "Life happens while you're making other plans." So, I'll just let life happen and see what comes up as my last dream comes true.

##

THE END